I0529663

Instapoet

A Novel

Thom Young/Matt Blythe

Instapoet

Copyright © 2018 Thom Young, Matt Blythe
All rights reserved.

No part of this publication may be reproduced, distributed,
or transmitted in any form or by any means, including
photocopying, recording, or other electronic or mechanical
methods, without the prior written permission of the
publisher, except in brief quotations embodied in critical
reviews, citations, and literary journals for noncommercial
uses permitted by copyright law.

This is a work of fiction. Names, characters, and incidents
either are the product of the author's imagination or are
used fictitiously, and any resemblance to events, or actual
persons—living or dead—is purely coincidental.

Satire is a sort of glass, wherein beholders do generally discover everybody's face but their own.

—*Jonathan Swift*

Table of Contents

Instapoet

One

"So that brings us to the age of Pelagius, and tomorrow we shall compare this age with its relationship to the works of literature of the period," Professor Andrews said, dismissing the class. His esteemed position was held at the bastion of literary integrity itself, Texas Tech University. It's located in the barren wasteland of West Texas with its sparse landscape of red dirt and the occasional caprock above the plains.

"What the hell is he talking about?" Max Wilson said, walking beside his friend, Jeff Button. They exited the lecture hall with the outline of large textbooks weighing in the bottom. It could seat up to five hundred students if need be, however, it was rarely filled.

"Fuck, if I know," Jeff said, looking at Max for some sort of witty reply, but his friend made none.

Both were in their senior year, with the end of college in sight. They had met in their freshman English class, taking notes on dangling modifiers and the proper use of an allusion. Jeff opted for a degree in Creative Writing while Max chose English, although his real path was an MFA degree.

"How is your submitting going?" Jeff asked.

"I got another one in *The Delinquent*," Max smiled knowing Jeff remained unpublished.

"Damn, how do you do it?" Jeff was never ceased to be amazed by Max and his growing list of publications.

"I'm a bit lucky I suppose, but you know I lay down a simple line and sometimes that's all it takes," Max said.

"Have you told Andrews about all this? Surely this could help your chances for candidacy in grad school?"

Max guffawed. "If only. Hell, I sent an email to my other professor about it. He's so laconic and uninterested in anything his students do, especially when they are low-grade magazines."

"So, it's a fucking rat-race, is what you're saying," Jeff inquired.

"Pretty much. You can try joining a clique, but all the *good ones* with connections are up north, like NYC and Boston. Good luck with that."

"Fuck. It's like, impossible to make anything," Jeff said, disgruntled.

The two men walked out of the building and into the early springtime air; brisk, but not completely frigid. Students donned in a motley of coats bustled back and forth along the crosswalks. They shook hands casually and parted ways for the afternoon. The next morning, they were to participate in a workshop, and both were tarrying behind on their manuscripts. Jeff returned to his apartment, which he shared with a few other students.

"Damn it, the fucking heat broke again? Some 'campus housing' this is!"

Jeff stomped from the door to his room. "Ok, barring any other major setbacks, time to write. But first—"

Jeff logged in and went to his Submit-arine account, an established platform for organizing literary submissions to various magazines. His computer, an obsolete Compack Gawkpad, whirred to life and began loading the page. The reason behind his lacking manuscript? Over 30 submissions that were marked 'In-progress'. He didn't want to break it to Max that he was submitting as well, so he kept it a secret. Nothing like a friendly competition.

"Finally, I can see some results. I believe I was supposed to hear back from—what the!"

Jeff was awestruck by the results that he saw. After waiting weeks on end for results, and his strange nuance of refreshing the site every two hours, he now saw many red 'Declined' labels.

"I guess the people have spoken. Let's see what kind of feedback I acquired."

Jeff slogged through sub after sub, checking off the generic responses from his list. 'Thank you for submitting...careful review...not a right fit at this time' rung in his head on repeat, mostly in a matter-of-fact way that an MFA grad would speak. But then, there was that *one* letter, —that was more than three lines long—that caught Jeff's attention. It was from *Tacky Xmas Sweater Collective*, a left-leaning online zine from the Newark area.

He meticulously devised a semi-autobiographical account of his youth experiences at the YMCA. He followed the guidelines, alluded to queer intentions, and included strong metaphors. The poem spanned four manuscript pages and he guaranteed to show them a thing or two, however, that was not the case. Upon the rejection letter, the editor left a conniving and pretentious response:

Dear Jeff Button,

Thank you for submitting 'Y Ma Contracted Aids'. Given the absurd quality of your manuscript, we were compelled to leave a most critical review on your complete and utter disrespect for the LGBTQIA+ community, as well as your patriarchal, misogynist, conservative-right locale and rhetoric. We at Tacky Xmas were in shock that an individual like yourself attempted to 'connect' with our audience through trite use of metaphors such as 'Ma's legs spread open when the flower bloomed in spring, thus smelling the nectar of a cryptic pistil.' and 'I saw a dick in the pool and the first thing I envisioned was Melville jerking off Captain Ahab.' This tongue-in-cheek attempt of a CIS, white (presumably) male relating to our gender-fluid collective will not be and shall NEVER be published in any future publications of Tacky Xmas. Our editor-in-chief called for your arrest, but alas, life sucks, and so does your poem.

With coldest regards,

—Tacky Xmas Sweater Collective

"Wow," Jeff shouted. "Do these yuppies even read Whitman or Ginsberg?" He rose from his desk chair, flipping over pencils and notebooks alike. "My bad for being satirical," he said, sarcastically, "Do all writers have to walk on eggshells? Or do people just think they are hot shit because they run a press? Y'know what? I should just create my own press! I bet I know more about poetry than any of these fools who write in these blogs!"

With that, Jeff began typing voraciously on the keyboard to Max. He had a splendid idea that was going to make waves, and this time, he was going to leave Melville out of the picture.

***

Max walked the four steps that led to Bledsoe Hall; the only remaining all men's dormitory on campus. There was no air conditioner which didn't mean much except for the months of August and September, where the Texas heat still reared its nasty head. The only solace about the dorm being it was attached to the women-only residence hall, Gaston. Max didn't have a serious girlfriend but lately, he had been seeing a woman named Julie Pinner. Her closeness provided the duality of nature; perhaps with more of a nod to Augustinian. That was the way Max thought of things now, with Anderson babbling on about the nature of mankind. It seemed a necessary evil to jump through on the way to an MFA.

However, the esteem made Max feel nauseous; in some way, it stood for everything he hated. The pomp of the elitist literary circles on campus basked in their failure one way or another, yet was conditioned to mask it. Some of them were published but they went about it the wrong way, using juvenile language and a pompous snobbery that Max disdained.

The truth is the graduate school had some clout, but the location of the university made it relatively unknown. Nobody gave two shits about the literary scene here, it was in the 'armpit' of Texas. It wasn't the 'big boys' on the East Coast with their publishing houses and funding courtesy of endowed grants.

The English department at Texas Tech now had their "Golden Boy", River Chang. Chang had won the Pushcart Prize last year and the professors were showering him in one collective gag fest; the MFA students practically worshipped him. Chang had released a chapbook, *My Ambition is a Golden Fallacy*, on the boorish *Silver Lake Press* and it had gotten rave reviews in the *The New Joker*. His most famous poem, "Whitman and A Machine Gun" had been a satirical take on the traditional values of middle America. Max hadn't met Chang yet, although he knew next year they would convene in graduate classes. If Chang wanted to slap the values of most Texans, then perhaps he could give him a taste of his own medicine. His ability to satire was also impressive and could formulate diatribes akin to the most prestigious prosecutor. Chang would have to wait, however, for when he reached his dorm room, there was a note that slid under the door.

What the hell are you doing? Everybody in the department read your satire piece on your blog. Did you not think we wouldn't see it? And guess who is teaching the workshop in the morning? River Chang. OMG. Anyways, we need to talk. Text me later.

Julie

Of course, the whole department had read his satirical piece. That was his intention. Max knew it might ruffle some feathers, especially of Dean Waters, whom Max had described as a 'plump table bird' with a 'moronic knowledge of literary analysis and creative writing'. Max made sure to degrade the senior readings as a remedial list of fodder for grade school children. This wasn't the first time he had poked fun at the English department, but perhaps he had pushed the envelope a bit far this time. Those things didn't bother Max, but knowing River Chang would be teaching his workshop in the morning, only added fuel to the dumpster fire the class itself already was.

Max's blog, "Dead Robots", was a very popular place for literary discussion and a destination to read his poetry and prose. In recent years, however, it drew less and less traffic with the advent of social media and its platform of 'community' with writing. Although it was a relatively new concept, hacks like Chang were using it to his advantage. Max disliked it but knew the crashing wave of the literary future pointed towards social media. He logged on his laptop computer and checked his email, noticing a message from Jeff which he briefly glanced at. "There's an idea", he thought. Next was his Submit-arine account and checked the list of accepted works. Max's list of publications, primarily in obscure magazines, had grown to over a hundred and even more if you counted the online zines. It wasn't something he wore like a badge of honor, but rather it had intrinsic value; a job was well done despite the years of rejection.

"I'll be damned," Max leaned back in his chair and felt a surge of giddiness come over him. His poem, "Red Apple," had been accepted in the *International Journal of Poetry*, one of the most prestigious literary magazines in the world. He was now in the club and even his professors, despite their efforts, had failed to get accepted in the International. It was the one everyone wanted to be in, and Max delighted in knowing his advantage. With a sinister grin on his face, contemplating how to disrupt the workshop, but also debated on even going to the workshop. He was well overdue for a beer. He logged off his laptop and texted Julie. He told her about his achievement, and soon everyone in the English department would know.

TWO

It was now 1 A.M.: the time when Jeff morphed into the curmudgeon that would ultimately plod through page after page of 12pt Times New Roman, double-spaced with 1" margins all-around and his 'trademarked' non-indented prose; the only slice of originality he possessed through his relatively uniform coursework. He knew that his creative writing professors were lenient on small nuances, but to Jeff, this was his ego. He had a quote posted on his wall which would stare him in the face every time he averted his gaze upward for a brief eye break:

The creative writer does the same as the child at play; he creates a world of fantasy which he takes very seriously.

—Sigmund Freud.

As to Freud's observation, he did indeed take his work seriously.

His current manuscript was a collection of poems in which he derived from various journals in his tenure at Texas Tech, albeit his best of the lot. He sniveled at the journals he brought from high school and the early semesters of college when gen-eds ruled his schedule and he believed himself to be a genius after a few social science courses. He assumed that a compacted thought with a trite metaphor would be his canonized and most studied work, however, his old work was far from perfect, let alone far from enjoyable.

A half-hour passed and the lingering caffeinated effects were dwindling on Jeff's psyche. He hated the gimmick of Adderall and the arguably poisonous concoction of energy shots, so he stuck to coffee and tea. He was nodding off, yet his fingers fought back, continuing to plod across the laptop surface, narrowly transcribing the written medium onto the screen.

"It's times like these where I can relate to any of the classic authors. Penning by candlelight, hell even moonlight, for hours on end. At least this quality I can uphold and grasp tightly," he muttered.

The rationalization of his humble typing did indeed encourage him, thus increasing his typing rate. It was an enlightening moment when he witnessed his thoughts flashing before him like lightning. He assumed the maestro of the chorus which was his mind; the single desk lamp seemed to flicker from the increase of neurological activity, manifesting a small electromagnetic field around his cranium. He assumed the mad scientist, like in previous works of M. Shelley and Hawthorne, in which he so avidly read, laughing maniacally at his creation through the veil of blood-burst eyes and exasperated, infrequent breathing. He felt clinically insane, knowing the deadline was close to 6 hours away.

Another half hour passed and it was complete. He immediately saved, printed dual sides, and shut his laptop. The clicking of the screen awoke him from his episode and he immediately plopped into his bed. He took a few glances at his phone and checked the emails from the bluish hue of the now darkened room. He deleted the spam and the came across an email from Max, three hours earlier.

I'm all in. Also, we can discuss the workshop tomorrow over beers. Rolling Rock as always. Max

"Fuck. Yes." Jeff said. The phone thumped onto his Modernist anthology textbook like a punch to the sternum.

***

"And that is how you properly write a Spenserian sonnet." River Chang said with a tinge of confidence He was admiring the starry-eyed coeds in the front row of the lecture hall. Chang was basking in his expertise in poetry instead of properly running a 'creative writing' workshop. Max slumped in the back row. He promised Jeff that he would turn in his manuscript since he copped-out from the waste of an hour.

"The best way to perhaps write a poem is to start out with something that relates to your life", Chang continued.

Max rolled his eyes. "Bullshit".

The class to erupt in laughter. Chang gasped and took a few steps back from the podium. The Golden Boy in a state of shock at the mere thought someone would criticize him after all, hadn't *he* won the Pushcart Prize and been the darling of *The New Joker*?

"That will be enough of that Mr. Wilson. Any more interruptions and you'll be asked to leave. Be respectful of our distinguished guest, please," Professor Andrews said.

"Isn't this a workshop? This feels more like a peer speaking down to a freshman intro class.

"Certainly, you are aware of Mr. Chang's credentials. He is more than qualified to lead this workshop."

"I believe that I'm the only one published in the International in here," Max said, quickly averting his gaze to Julie a few rows down. She was staring up at him with disdain in her eyes. "I guess the news hasn't spread?"

"While that is an admirable accomplishment, it has nothing to do with conducting a workshop. However, if you interrupt my class again, perhaps a meeting with Dean Waters can solve any issue you may be having." Andrews gave the ultimatum. He put a hand on River Chang's shoulder. He was shaking a bit. "Sorry, dearest friend. You may continue the workshop."

Max didn't say a word and sunk back into his seat. The remainder of the workshop, he remained silent but knew the entire department would be watching him the rest of the semester. He texted Jeff and told him to meet at Crickets, a craft beer pub close to campus, during happy hour. Max liked Jeff's idea, perhaps it might be the perfect catalyst to bring some life to the exasperated literary scene.

Three

Max arrived around 5:15 PM and gazed around the dim bar. The college's colors donned the ceiling and the upper portion of the walls; wainscot of hearty maple lined the lower. Many high-tops crowded around the hearty oak bar. There were signs of life, in both clothing attire and spirit; the baseball team was on a five-game win streak. Max spotted Jeff in a corner booth with his laptop covering the lower portion of his face. Given his furrowed brow, he could only imagine that Jeff was muttering obscenities to himself.

"Yo, dude!" Max yelled.

Jeff waved him over. He had papers all over, with various colors of ink, and a quart of beer, which was about three-quarters finished.

"What are you drinking?" Max said, sitting down with his coat to the side.

"Some beer from New York. Called Brooklyn Lager."

A female server, roughly the age of fifty, strutted by and saw Max without a drink.

"Hello sweetie. What can I get you?"

"Double Deuce of Rolling Rock, please."

"I'll have another lager," Jeff added.

"You got it!"

Max turned to Jeff, "If only she knew what happened earlier, I think she would need to use a different noun."

The next round arrived shortly. The two friends clinked glasses.

"You should've seen the horror on Chang's face today. You missed one hell of a performance!" Max gloated.

"I got an email from a friend in that class. Called you 'a buck-wild skeptic'. You sure know how to ruffle those feathers."

"Thanks, man. I'm sure that next week we will have a workshop *without* a guest." Max guzzled a quarter of his mug. "Let me see this new 'idea' you've been crafting, Jeff."

"Here are the specifications of my idea. The blog, which I developed on BlogSpot, mind you, is fully functional and ready to receive payments."

Max scanned it. "What is it?"

Jeff groaned. "It's my idea of a publishing company! Can't you tell?"

"I mean," Max grimaced, "I can see the basic idea, but it seems too vague. You have the name of the company backgrounded by this frivolous logo that looks like a crazy metal band logo. Also, what's the music? Shouldn't it have a menu bar?"

"Well, that's the point! Draw them in with simplicity so that they are encouraged to view the website in its entirety! All about the clicks, man. That's another way of making money."

"Ok. Let me try it out."

Max took the laptop and started clicking away. After a few minutes, and a quizzical stare, he turned it back around.

"All the links seem to loop around and around. I couldn't even get an email support. Are you sure this is the final draft?"

"Yes. Max. This is how it will work," Jeff said, burping immediately after. He was drunk, or sleep deprived, or both. "The point is to make the site so captivating, that there is no need for 'uniformity'. Think of it as a circle. Plus, when they read the mission statement, people will know this is the real deal. Who needs $10 submission fees with a 99% chance of a decline, when you can get an *entire* manuscript published for a small flat-rate fee?"

"Jeff, not to sound like a dick, but $498.99 is a lot of money. Sounds like a cash cow."

"What do you mean?" Jeff gleamed with contempt.

"Well, you know that Andrews will call you a capitalist pig for one. Two, what are you going to do with all this money? Who's your target audience?"

"Well…well," Jeff became flustered, "I want to go to grad school! Here I am, offering top-notch literary criticism and editorial services for other starving artists like myself, in exchange for a low, and I mean, a *low* fee that can be paid monthly via credit card or cashier's check and—"

"That's all fine and dandy but, who is going to buy into this?"

Jeff paused. For once, he was unsure.

"I don't know yet, Max. Other undergrads? Current grad students? Once they see what good a service I am performing for the community, the more it will snowball."

"Got'ya."

Both men drank gratuitously and reset.

"Well, I must say I wish you luck. I know where your heart is, and I know you're quite talented in both writing and criticism. Hope you get some business soon," Max held up the remnants of his mug. "Cheers?" Jeff, with a sheepish smile on his face, raised his glass and clinked again; his glass dark brown and Max's pale yellow. It was a contrasting sight, nonetheless.

***

It was around 8 when Max bid his friend goodbye, although good riddance often seemed the more suitable salutation when dealing with Jeff. Although Max entertained implementing his best friend's plan, which essentially was nothing more than a vanity press, Max couldn't help but think of its inherent fallacy. Who would buy into the crap? Was there actually a target market for this swindle? A legion of morons lining up to buy while Jeff pilfered their parents' credit card numbers. The carefree undergraduates that wanted nothing more than international fame from their mediocre poetry, and perhaps that in itself was the genius of Jeff's dubious plan?

Max pondered these things thinking of the monetary aspect and considering the rising cost of graduate school, anything seemed fair game; a means to an end. While the Machiavellian side of things worked practically, was it not also fair to question the ethical side? The old Pelagian versus Augustine debate and the mantra of the imbecile himself: Anderson. Max tried to block the sound of his least favorite professor from his head, but it seemed a lost cause. He lay down on the bed and heard his phone vibrate

Hey got to finish this paper before my first class tomorrow come over and help? Love Julie

"Another lusty text, eh?"

Julie, like most of the women he dated, had devious plans to get something she wanted, and often it meant getting her carnal desires satisfied or using them to further her agenda. Max replied, reluctantly at first, knowing what the night held. He would end up writing her whole paper then would embark on an escapade in the sack. There had to be an agreement, some sort of compromise. Max grabbed his cigarettes and made the short jaunt over to Gaston Hall. When he arrived at Julie's room, she greeted him at the door in a sports bra and panties. She did have a defined body, in fact.

"Glad you came, I can always count on my love," Julie smiled and wrapped her arms around Max's neck. She pecked him on the lips.

"Where is your laptop? No time to waste, woman," Max nudged Julie away and walked over to the desk.

"Well, it's nice to see you too."

"What is the topic of your paper?" Max stared at a blank computer screen with a title that read, 'Research Paper'.

"Are you fucking kidding me? What idiotic class is this for? I suppose your generic title is par for this remedial education? What exactly is the subject matter?"

"I have the notes," Julie said, handing the pages over.

"Let's see…'The Malthusian influence on postmodern literature'. An exciting thesis indeed, and you expect me to bang out fifteen pages for you before dawn?"

"I knew you would understand this, you know all this shit," Julie said, rubbing Max's back as he sat.

"I can write this in my sleep, which is what I feel coming on," Max said, gloating.

"So, you'll do it?"

"If you want me to write a paper, then I shall oblige. Is this for Greene's class?"

"Yes, thank you! I'm going to nap. Wake me up when you're done."

Max got to work after cracking a beer.

Malthus was a complete and utter asshole. His theory is not only moronic but properly aligned with the professor and content of this asinine class. Perhaps you should be the one explaining to your 'mullet fish eyed students' what a complete waste of money and time their undergraduate education truly is….

"Fifteen more pages," Max said aloud. "All for Greene…" The TV in the corner was repeating trashy reality TV shows, which made his job even worse. He ultimately tuned out the noise and put his head down.

***

Max jotted a few sources then saved the paper. He saw that Julie was already logged on her student email account, so he attached the PDF and sent it.

"Julie, wake up. All finished, and I sent it to Greene."

"Oh, you're the best," she replied, sheepishly. In her sleep, a bra-string slid down her shoulders. The other one came off. "Maybe, I can make it up to you, hmm?"

"Nonsense. What's done is done. Plus, you gave me the beer."

Max got up from the desk and began to walk towards the door.

"Wait, don't go."

Julie rushed to Max and embraced him.

"It's really, no—" Max mumbled.

Julie began kissing him, embracing his hearty chest. A misplaced hand slid down to his crotch.

"Oops, that's not my pen," She said, winking.

"Oh, why the hell not?"

He picked Julie up and took her to the bedroom. He tossed her on the bed and ripped off what little clothes remained. It didn't take long. He gave her a few hearty thrusts, ramming her head into the headboard. The oldest dance in the book. Max wiped off, dressed, and left without saying a word. Julie sat up in bed trying to remember if she took her birth control. She got lost in the heat of the moment; her flesh had gotten the best of her. She tried to comfort herself, knowing the possibility of the unknown often led to the unwanted. Julie did know one thing: Max was an asshole, yet she liked it, a lot.

"Just couldn't help myself," he said, walking back to his dorm. "If I wasn't so damn tired, maybe I'd stay longer."

Four

Dean Waters took a deep breath after reading a slew of emails and surveyed the many framed awards and degrees that hung above his desk. There was his undergraduate degree from Penn and nestled above sat his Masters from Harvard. The crowning jewel of the collection was his Doctorate in Linguistics and English Literature from USC. Yet despite his accolades and publications, he found himself at Texas Tech in Lubbock, Texas. A city that viewed progress as an albatross which hung on its red neck. Lubbock remained segregated and most of the students were as 'lily white' as the snow that covered the caprock in the dead of winter. Who did he piss off to end up in a place like this?

He dreamed of tenure in the Ivy League, but the cruel world put him in charge of a department of listless professors and dimwitted students. The addition of River Chang brought a glimmer of hope, but to Waters, it seemed a drop in the bucket of mediocrity. Waters reached over and grabbed the phone on his desk.

"Greene, this is Waters. What the hell are you teaching in your class? Do you care to explain this young lady's research paper? This Julie Pinner? Is that her name?"

"I forwarded you the email because of my deep concern. Ms. Pinner has personally insulted me and you as representatives of this esteemed department. Did you have time to peruse her paper?" Greene waited with baited breath for Waters' reply.

"I read the damn paper, and let me say the quality of writing is outstanding. I might commend you for that, although I believe you had nothing to do with this young lady's writing ability. What concerns me is the scathing style of the paper, it demonstrates that your students are not mastering the content in your class."

"But, surely, one student shouldn't speak for my instruction; most of my students demonstrated a mastery of the content on their papers."

"Nonsense, Greene. I want you to tell Ms. Pinner to meet with me tomorrow during your class. I want to hear exactly what is going on in your class, and why she wrote a brilliant paper that viciously destroyed your teaching."

"That's preposterous, and you know it." Greene slammed down the phone causing a nice clang in Water's ear.

"So that's how it's going to be. Perhaps Ms. Pinner can be the spark to get rid of Greene once and for all."

***

Max released a chapbook a few years ago, *Cow Dung and Murder*. The sales were dismal, but it got rave reviews on several lit blogs and in university literary magazines. His publisher even placed the chapbook on Shamazon, but it failed to make a splash in any of the poetry rankings. If anything, Max prided himself on being a published poet unlike so many of his peers with nothing but an MFA in their eyes. If there was a thorn in Max's foot, it was the online lit blog, "WANK". Max always laughed at the name, the nomenclature appropriate for the 'snobbish wankers' that communed there.

Their literary magazine, *Pride,* was ranked in the top fifty by the Pushcart Prize. Max disdained the Pushcart mainly because he had never been nominated; just another in the East Coast club. Max submitted, but knew its editor, Lisa Polk, carried a personal vendetta against him. Max routinely posted his rants against WANK and all its contributors on their community discussion board. While this perhaps kept him from gracing the pages, he wouldn't compromise on what he deemed injustice to the written word.

Max got on his laptop and perused their webpage. He browsed the community discussion board until he saw a post by Lisa Polk herself. Max couldn't believe it, she had gone too far this time. A personal attack against him and his chapbook; a link to a one-star review on Shamazon without a 'verified purchase'. *This meant war.*

Max retrieved his favorite pen which he nicknamed 'Revenge'. If Lisa wanted to fire the first shot, she could expect a total annihilation. "Oh, angel trumpet swoon," Max thought. He began what would become his treatise. A post on the discussion board would not suffice, Max would pen a handwritten letter and mail it personally to Lisa Polk. Max envisioned the pompous editor sitting behind her desk, reading what would become the obligatory final nail in the coffin. *Game. Set. Match.*

Max wiped the sweat from his forehead and pulled down his Chicago Cubs' cap to eye level. His blood began to boil, reaching a feverish temperature which begged to turn red upon seeping through his vengeful skin. Max paused a minute to gather his thoughts, noticing his white flabby gut protruding over his gray sweatpants like Moby Dick caught in Ahab's net. Was this the price to pay for his attempt at being an immortal poet? A complete 'letting go' of his physical wellbeing? The empty Rolling Rock bottles and full ashtrays hinted at an early demise, but nothing could crush his spirit, for it danced with the gods, an undeterred will that would make Stalin blush like a schoolgirl. Max took a deep breath, summoning Lucifer himself, and began to write.

Dear Great Whore of Babylon,

The unprovoked rebuke of myself and beloved chapbook must have made your frigid heart dance in the stench that is your putrid collective of moronic thought known as WANK and said sewer rag "Pride'. What surely is a rebuke to the age of Pelagius, you embrace Augustine of Hippo with poisonous Jezebel lips. What shall I do for such an abomination? Call down fire to lick up Baal? No. I'm but a mere man in the shadow of Adam's original sin tempted by Eve (the first harlot) preceded by Lilith's seductive beauty. It's always the weaker sex that casts the die of misfortune, isn't it? I can envision you nodding in agreement, as you sit behind a disgraceful editorial desk, one that sums up your failure as a writer. Perhaps that's your pinnacle of glory? I will leave no stone unturned in my treatise against everything you and your swine publication stand for, hence the transparent introduction you just read. Where shall I commence? It began one autumn night on the dregs of the internet....

Five

In the days that followed, Jeff became a hermit, and not just on the fact that finals were approaching; he wanted no distractions at all. His roommates would knock every 6 hours on his door, just to assure that he was still alive. "Damn fools," he would mutter as the unmelodic knocks would stir his laser focus. "They disappear for term after term, *now* they want some attention."

"Yo, brah, you good in there?"

"Jeff!"

"Guys! I am quite alright!" Jeff shouted. "I'm pissing in water jugs and have plenty of gluten-free trail mix to last me to next semester."

"Alright. You wanna hit this?"

"Hit what? The side of your head maybe when I slap the shit out of you."

"This cross-joint bro," the roommates said while chuckling. "Took us like 2 hours to make, brah."

Jeff, despite having chaste virtues in keeping his body mentally and physical organic, rationalized that a little bit of weed couldn't have been so bad. He exited the room, slowly at first. He gazed through the ½" slat made by the jamb, darted his already bloodshot eyes, and deemed it clear enough to exit. He transitioned from his bland room into a billowing cloud of hemp. Did he return to his work? Nope.

Five hours passed by and the sun comfortably rose upon the horizon. Jeff was intolerant to the drug; it took but a few gratuitous puffs to make him pass out. It was now 7 AM and his grand scheme was impeded for yet another day. He awoke on his floor, cursed briefly, but his mind was clear and ready to begin the day. He was scheduled to sit-in on a career seminar at nine, in which he was to give a testimony on his time spent at Texas Tech. There was something in the air that morning which made him extremely peppy and upbeat. He wasn't quite sure either, but once the professor walked in the door of that seminar, he was aware of what he was going to do.

"Welcome students to the career seminar. We have a few honored guests that will be speaking to you today. After each presenter, we will open the room up for question and answer," The adjunct spoke with the demeanor of a mouse begging for cheese if mice could in fact talk. Jeff yawned. He spotted a chair next to a woman. They regarded each other with a brief smile. Jeff was confident enough with his dimples.

"How many speakers are there?" Jeff whispered.

"Uh, three, I think. I didn't get a good look," the student said. Her voice peaked at a higher octave than he expected, even in a whisper.

"This will be fun," Jeff said.

"Why?"

"You'll see."

"What year are you?"

"Senior. You?"

"Same," she giggled. "Seems a bit too late for you, huh?"

"Maybe. Maybe not," Jeff said confidently. "I have a few ideas up my sleeve."

"Like?"

"Just wait. I have a few questions for—" Jeff squinted at the whiteboard, "Mr. Francis McDonnell."

"You seem very intuitive," she said, now turning to face the first presenter, silent upon the podium. He was gathering his notes.

Jeff didn't respond.

Francis McDonnell droned on about irrelevant material for well over thirty minutes. Jeff, who was still under the aftereffects of the marijuana, finally succumbed to dreariness. The seminar was packed with about 200 doe-eyed students, well now 199 given that Jeff fell asleep. By the time Jeff awakened, Mr. McDonnell vacated the stand and yet another academic arrived. He was younger and donned a Texas Tech hoodie.

"Is he a student?" Jeff muttered. The female peer he spoke to earlier was awestruck. "You don't know *him*? He's the president of *Stone Pony Literary Review*! Francesco Carmichael."

"Um, okay?" Jeff questioned.

"It's Texas Tech's own!"

Jeff assumed a pretentious smirk. "Oh, *them*. I may have slung some drafts to them back in the day, but they are just not my type of audience."

"Ok, whatever you say," the woman said, frowning. Once her eyes locked upon the tall, slender man with lush combed-over hair, she returned to a stupor.

"Ugh, what is it with these women and asshats like him?" Jeff thought. He listened to the presenter's introduction.

"Hello, my fellow classmen. If you don't know me— but most likely you have heard of me—I am Francesco Carmichael, Editor-in-Chief of Stone Pony."

"Ugh, what a twatwaffle. Let me guess: a journalism major?"

"—and I am a senior journalism major."

"Ha, fucking knew it," Jeff smiled. Despite his seven-inch long auburn brown beard, he already assumed the high ground.

"So, let me ask you all. Who here has submitted to Stone Pony?"

About fifty people raised their hand. Jeff groaned, raising his hand for giggles. The woman beside him, now quite cheeky, raised her hand so high, she had to extend her fingertips to appear the highest. Her chest was pushed out. Jeff realized her ploy, yet was starved for promiscuity, passing his eyes toward her. She didn't notice, but he imagined her jade eyes befalling him, accompanied by furrowed brows and ample chastising.

"Nice, very nice. We at Stone Pony appreciate all that you have to offer us and Texas Tech. If you could all just please keep your hands arisen while my secretary takes count. We are using it for records; my successor is being combed with a fine tooth."

"Now he is reminding me of Bill Clinton," Jeff continued to think. He did, however, keep his hand raised, but it began to rescind. The secretary finished her tally. All the hands dropped. Francesco clasped his hands together and breathed in a gratuitous breath.

"For all that have not submitted, I do implore you to gather your best work and to submit to our exclusive 'Dog Days Edition'! Submissions close in exactly one week, and it will be my final publication as editor-in-chief. I plan on using this edition to spearhead my graduate career and would love for my future professors to read all of your marvelous poetry and fiction!"

"Look at this schmuck, spinning his narrative around his fucking finger," Jeff said.

"Ahem, is there something I said that offended you, sir?" Francesco said, staring directly at Jeff.

"To be frank, I've been roasting you in my head this entire time, but this one accidentally slipped out. Oh well, here we are. What's up?"

"May I ask what grade level you are? Or better yet, are you even a student? Or did you roll in with the tumbleweeds?" Francesco snickered. The hall turned to face Jeff. Some laughed quietly.

"Senior," Jeff muttered.

"You look like Socrates mixed with Eddie Vedder, yet have the former's looks and lack the latter's talent!" Francesco mocked. More of the room laughed now. Jeff rose abruptly from his seat, now appearing to be engaged in a form of Greek apology.

"Listen here, frivolous Fran. I knew from the second week of my freshman year that your magazine was trash, but I gave you a chance. I submitted a wonderfully acute Wordsworth tribute 'From the Grotto of my Fallen Lord' right before Thanksgiving break. I received a completely bullshit response to my seven-page piece. "It's too long. We require brevity" blah, blah, blah. You could've serialized between two editions but no."

"Oh, I do remember that piece, yes. I was wondering why the pen name was 'Glenn Gigglesworth'. I had many a laugh at your triteness."

"Jokes on you, asshole," Jeff was shouting, "I had it published in the Missouri Review. My one and only published piece. How's that for accreditation, fucker?"

The lecture hall gasped. Francesco remained at the podium; a balled fist holding his notes down firmly. Jeff gathered his bag.

"You'll see, all of you! Once I get out of this hellhole, I am going to start my own magazine. You won't know what hit ya. It'll be the next best read since Fahrenheit 451. Just you wait, Frannie!"

Jeff stormed out of the room, along with sparse others, including the woman next to him. It was unclear if she was enraged by Jeff remarks, or was awakened to the farcical facade that Francesco had promoted. Whichever her motive, she rushed behind the stammering Jeff and tapped him on the shoulder. He turned slowly and was greeted with a stinging slap to his gnarly cheek. The woman's face was beet red, and so was Jeff's.

"You! You," the woman stammered. Her palm was also red with fury. Her chest was engorged and her skin appeared to harm one that would caress its porous surface. She had a dermal anchor on her sternum.

"Are," Jeff responded calmly. He was too flustered to even think. His body tiptoed closer to the woman.

"Such!"

"A!"

"Fucking marvelous bastard!" the woman screamed before plowing her lips into Jeff. Both parties transformed into a sweating mess of anonymous love.

Jeff was on the brink of voracity; the tile floor was prime for an intense lay. However, he gathered whatever wit was left within his being and spoke.

"Come with me to my dorm."

"Yes, yes, I will," she said firmly and attentively.

Both parties dashed away from the scene, leaving all wanderers scratching their heads in astonishment. Within ten minutes, Jeff took her on his cluttered mattress. Not even the bust of Edgar Allan Poe batted an eyelash to the monstrosity that the couple formed. If anything, the affair was true poetry in motion.

Six

Dean Waters minimized his favorite porn site, "College Girls Gone Wild", and answered his desk telephone.

"Dean Waters...oh...yes, send Ms. Pinner in right away." Waters straightened up a few papers on his desk, although he wasn't sure why, however, the image of his self-importance went a long way in academia. Julie entered and stood rigidly by the door.

"Ms. Pinner, do sit down and thank you for the meeting. I hope you're not too disappointed in missing out on Professor Greene's class today." Waters said. He chuckled at the thought of Greene.

"No, it's not a problem at all."

"I guess you know why we're meeting today? Did Greene tell you?"

"No, he didn't, just that you wanted to see me."

"It concerns your research paper, the one titled, "Malthus and His Moronic Thoughts". Does that sound familiar?"

"I, uh. Yes, I suppose that is my paper." Julie winched and sat up straight in her chair.

"I'm not here to chastise you, Ms. Pinner. The topic of your paper is fascinating and I must admit it's some of the best writing I've ever seen from an undergraduate. You should be commended for such brilliance, and despite Professor Greene giving you a failing grade, I asked him to give you an 'A' on the paper. Splendidly written Julie, just magnificent. I can call you Julie, right?"

"Yes…but…you see I—" Julie hesitated to tell the truth about the paper.

"Don't worry about what Professor Greene thinks, you should be proud of your commended writing ability. It's a bit early, but if you have the ambition to pursue the MFA program, I will give you the highest recommendation."

"That's nice of you, but honestly I haven't thought that far off." Julie squirmed in her seat inching her mini skirt up.

"Oh yes, more, my lovely." Waters thought. He envisioned a seductive encounter just now.

"Dean Waters? Are you alright?"

"Oh yes, excuse me, Ms. Pinner, a bit of a fainting spell. You know how stressful my job can be sometimes, being responsible for our distinguished department is no easy task."

"I bet it isn't, is that all you wanted to see me about?"

"Actually no, I wanted to ask you about Professor Greene's class. How do you feel about it? Are you learning anything? Do you approve of his teaching style? Is it primarily direct instruction?"

"I don't know really, maybe I'm not qualified to say."

"Let's say you were asked to evaluate Professor Greene based on his teaching ability, hypothetically of course, what would you grade him?"

"I don't know, he lets us do workshops which I enjoy."

"It sounds to me like he isn't doing enough direct instruction, I can see a little disappointment in your eyes." Waters smiled at Julie hoping she would take her skirt off.

"I don't know…you see…" Julie shimmied in her seat.

"Nonsense, you're a brilliant writer. I will make note of your dissatisfaction with Professor Greene's instructional methods. That will be all, Ms. Pinner."

"Thank you," Julie said. She felt trapped, beholden to Max for writing her paper, and now Dean Waters was putting words in her mouth. That wasn't her only concern. Max hadn't texted her in days, and something told her their relationship was purely sexual. *That bastard.* As she exited his office, she immediately texted him, throwing apprehension to the ground.

***

Henry Andrews had been a professor at Texas Tech for nearly twenty years, and with retirement in sight, he needed to make it through two more semesters. He had seen many quality writers among his students over the years, but one stuck out: eccentric slacker Max Wilson. What bothered Andrews the most was that Max rarely did assignments unless they were exams and research papers which accounted for a majority of his grade. It was frustrating but worse than that, was Max's attitude, which seemed to be arrogant at best. He was willing to speak to Dean Waters to hopefully settle the score.

"Dean Waters, this is Professor Andrews. I hope I'm not disrupting you from anything."

Waters minimized the porn on his computer. "Not at all, what's on your mind?"

"This may not seem like an issue, but there's a certain student within the department that I need to make you aware of. His name is Max Wilson."

"That name seems familiar…what do I need to know about him?"

"Namely, it's his attitude in my class. He berates me in front of the other students and the other day he insulted River Chang during my workshop."

"Insulted *Chang*? This will not be tolerated, the last thing we need is our Golden Boy transferring. I want you to keep an eye on this Max, and if this happens again, immediately send him to me. I can see about getting him expelled if his shenanigans continue."

"Excellent, there's one more thing, and it's a bit of a rumor, but some of the undergraduates have mentioned that Max has been writing other students' papers for them."

"It looks like we might have a case of academic fraud on our hands." Waters said, licking his lips. His favorite thing was expelling insubordinate students.

"There's no proof of course, but some of the students said it happened in Greene's class."

"Greene? I wouldn't worry about him much longer. He told me he might be taking a sabbatical next year, but let's keep this between us." Waters leaned back in his chair and opened 'College Girls Gone Wild' on his computer, keeping the call active.

"I won't say a thing, thanks for listening to my concerns."

"This is very important, and like I said keep an eye on Max Wilson. In a positive note, we have a rising star among our undergraduates."

"Who's that?"

"I talked to a very bright young lady yesterday. Do you know Julie Pinner?"

"I think so, but with all of my students it's tough to know them all."

"She's a real whiz with the written word and a prime candidate for our MFA program. I am impressed with her writing, plus she's a real looker."

Waters fantasized for a minute then continued, "I'm telling you, her and Chang could really put us on the map in the literary circles."

"Outstanding, I will seek her out and formally introduce myself."

"Thank you, Andrews, you can call me—"

"What's that noise? Sounds like…giggling?"

Waters hurriedly clicked the mouse, pausing the video.

"Oh, I don't know. Must be something going on outside. Lots of students out and about."

"Thank you for speaking with me, Dean Waters."

Waters hung up the phone and grabbed a Cuban from his desk drawer. He lit it up and then watched two naked coeds mud wrestle on the glowing screen, surrounded by young men with red plastic cups in their hands.

"Close one."

Seven

Max saw his phone illuminate as he took a draw on a green-hued bottle of Rolling Rock. He often drank alone, unless Jeff offered to buy a few rounds at the pub.

"What is it now?" Max thought to himself seeing that Julie had texted him. The message said they needed talk as soon as possible.

"A lusty wench, a strumpet the likes of which hasn't been seen since Solomon's concubines," Max said as he typed in the security code to access his laptop. "Women have been the downfall of man for centuries, an apocalypse if you will, and all for something between her legs. Surely this is how Rome fell, perhaps all wars could be blamed on the female species, mankind caught in a universal conundrum of wanting them, yet knowing the dire consequences."

Max pondered his thoughts, then let out a belch any frat boy would have been proud of if Max dabbled in such juvenile pursuits. He didn't like the idea of buying friends, and the mere thought of it upset his gastrointestinal system.

Max turned off his phone, with no intention of responding to Julie. He browsed a few of his favorite literary sites purposely avoiding "WANK" until his treatise was completely done. He wasn't even halfway done with it, yet he felt it needed something that he couldn't quite put his finger on.

Max visited the mother of all literary magazine sites, *Poetry Review*. This was the journal Pulitzer winners were in, and though Max hated to admit it, its prestige was greater than what he was used to. Bukowski himself couldn't even grace its pages until after his death, and only because his widow raised a stink. There didn't seem to be anything interesting on the site today, a few tributes to Victorian-era poets, and a glorification of the Romanticism period. The subject bored Max so he scrolled down to read about the featured 'poet of the day'. Max couldn't believe his eyes. It was none other than River Chang. There was the Golden Boy's picture complete with his bio and two of his poems.

"Blasphemy. What idiotic shit. The end of the world must be nigh," Max said as he read Chang's poems. "What a disgrace, nothing more than a polished turd with haiku tendencies."

Max realized nobody could hear him talking to himself. His rage began to build. What bothered him the most was that Chang bested him and Max would not tolerate being second. He had plans for Chang; the roots of which began to churn in his melon-sized noggin. Max continued working on his treatise against WANK and the harlot Lisa Polk, but he wasn't pleased with it. There was something missing, perhaps not enough vitriol, but Max knew he couldn't rush perfection. In the meantime, a peculiar literary phenomenon was sweeping through the MFA program like herpes. The rise of social media poetry had become the new rave on popular sites like Bumbler and Glanceagram. Max couldn't help but laugh at the putrid "she poetry" that so many of the worthless hacks were posting to the delight of their idiotic followers and fans. It was the antithesis of all that was poetry. "What a perfect mirror of our society, a true mantra of the morons," Max thought.

To make matters even worse the Golden Boy himself had created a profile on Glanceagram. River Chang had over thirty thousand followers and his popularity seemed to grow by the day. They did it strictly for likes and followers. They could easily fit on a cellphone screen and were more often composed of calligraphy fonts for visual appeal.

The hatred began to boil deep within Max's bowels, creating a flatulence stench that seemed to leak anytime he was around the English department. If Chang thought he would be the only Glanceagram 'pop-poet', he was going to get the surprise of a lifetime. Max knew what to do and the wheels began to churn in his brain. He had something so genius that he couldn't help but laugh, and all he had to do was take care of a few other things first.

Max's phone vibrated. It was a text from Julie. Max didn't feel like dealing with her crap. The text was humorous, it seemed Julie was acting like a damsel in distress. Max laughed and tossed his phone on the bed, but her message resonated in his mind.

I think Greene knows you wrote my paper...text me ASAP

That was going to be the least of Julie's concerns, by the time Max got done with her. Max knew a few things about Dean Waters that might help his cause; that being the destruction of the Texas Tech English Department. He knew if anyone was willing to help him it would be Jeff, and although his friend hadn't mentioned it, they were on the same page. The more he thought about it, Max didn't want to pursue the MFA. The fact being Max didn't need a graduate degree in something he already conquered. His writing was published all over the world, beating his peers when it came to being published in the prestigious literary journals. The days of facing rejection were over and now anyone with a smartphone could be an overnight sensation.

"How dare they destroy the true craft of the written word. Such a blasphemy to the arts," Max thought, debating on gulping down another beer, but he decided on another route, at least for now. He grabbed his phone and downloaded Glanceagram with baited breath. He signed up for a new account and found some of the idiots in the English department. Max smiled looking at his username; it was genius. *Tyler Young.*

Max found River Chang and followed him. Max would remain a 'ghost account' with no profile picture or any posts. That would soon change, however, and it would be a poetic war the likes of which the platform had never seen. The devious plan had commenced and there was hell coming with it.

"That was easy," Max said. "Now back to my treatise."

Julie texted him numerous times, but she wasn't getting the picture. After a good hour or so, Max pushed away from his computer and admired his handiwork. It was a magnificent finale.

You have spread your legs for the literary world, and its putrid stench has come home to roost. Oh, the age of Augustine hath reared its pious head.

With the treatise to his satisfaction, Max organized the fifty plus pages. He took a safety pin from the desk drawer and pricked the inside of his arm, then signed his name in blood on the last page. Max addressed it to Lisa Polk c/o WANK magazine and sealed his masterpiece. In a few weeks, he would stick it in the mail and await Armageddon.

In his frenzy of a diatribe, Max forgot all about attending class, and to make matters worse Julie had been blowing up his phone like a cluster bomb. This matter didn't concern him, so he grabbed his phone and searched for images of guys with beards that looked like 'hipsters'. It would be the perfect profile picture on Glanceagram. The tween and teen fangirls would lick it up like a Bachelor marathon on a lazy Sunday. He uploaded the best one he could find and finished up his profile. He was now the bohemian poet, Tyler Young. He perused the catalog of poems within the app to write something similar.

"Yeesh," Max sighed, looking at the monotonous batch of work that seemed to recycle itself after ever few scrolls. With enough research—or lack thereof— he posted his first she poem. Max knew the most popular poetry hashtags would give it a leg up and he tagged the reality starlet, Karen Kramer. It was a longshot, but desperate times called for chasing after the masses. Max couldn't help but laugh when he saw his first post.

She is she.

***

Julie sat at her desk in silence. She watched the rain outside pound the window and a sense of melancholia came over her. She honestly loved Max, but lately, it seemed all he did was ignore her. She felt strangely turned on because it was a challenge. The other albatross around her neck had been all the praise Dean Waters had heaped on her for the paper Max wrote. She was being proclaimed a genius within the department and the other students were congratulating her. She felt awful living a lie, but there was no turning back. Julie began to think Max tricked her on purpose. After all his nature was devious at its best.

Julie thought about her options: keep living a lie or confess to her peers and the faculty that her paper was fraudulent. The ability to easily transition to graduate school and likely excel made it all seem worth it. But what if, even then, her façade was taken apart? Texas Tech would disown her, knowing that she conned her way to the top. She knew Max didn't care, but what if he were to blackmail her?

"Maybe all I needed was to write it myself, then none of this would've happened, even if it was bad," she said.

A crash of lightning startled her, and so did the rumbling thunder. Her notes and pens shook from the shockwave. The thoughts raced through her mind and there was no way out.

Eight

J eff awoke to the image of a sleepy woman in his bed; her hair was messy and blotted her eyes from the impending moonlight peeking around the blackout blinds. This was not a dream. He wasn't used to a roommate, let alone a lover. He hadn't had another human in his bed since his freshman year, and even that experience was short-lived. For some reason or another, Jeff elected to a higher tuition rate for room and board in lieu of 'mandatory dorm sharing'. Not even the admissions counselors could understand why he chose that. Jeff would identify his solemnity to that of an alpha wolf. It was only this term, his final, in which he was heavily peer pressured into rooming with four other guys of various ages—also the fact that Jeff had long estranged from his family after he made his decision to change his major.

He was running thin on a meager $500 scholarship from a local bank he received in the winter, and his refusal to work left him with no other choice but to ration and to figuratively squander off the other guys. They were below him in intellect and from affluent families who sprinkled their every whim with checks and 'care packages' to their door. No matter if it was a fully furnished Thanksgiving leftover, to Bubba Burgers in family value packs, Jeff's rhetoric and argumentative skills allowed him a cut; always. His stomach growled. Business as usual.

Jeff stirred lightly to avoid waking his beautiful mistress. He heard not a sound from behind his bedroom door. The louts were most likely passed out from yet another vulgarity-laden night.

"What time is it?" Jeff groaned.

The woman stirred. Her hand removed the hair from her face as she unclosed her eyes. Those beautiful orbs that saw Jeff as the peak of intellectual prowess still mewed for him in post-coital bliss.

"Hey babe," she spoke softly. "I'm so hungry. You wore me out."

Jeff sat at the edge of the bed, unresponsive at first.

"Wanna' grab some food?" she asked. "Diner is open I bet."

He remained facing the wall, legs dangling off his heavily worn full-size bed. Somehow, the box-spring was still intact. No headboard either, but he minded her fragile head earlier in the night with his forearm wrapped gingerly around her like a crown. He just wanted her to leave; to skedaddle into the night so he can absolve himself in silence. But this wasn't business as usual.

"Ok. Get dressed."

***

The couple entered the diner to a bombastic, late-semester crowd. Her arm interlaced within his, like a nostalgic portrayal of Depression-era chivalry. The waitress, a middle-aged woman with thinning blond hair and a sweaty brow, glanced at them anxiously, gauging the size of their party behind them. Another group entered.

"Just us, ma'am," Jeff said without the sharp, neurotic tone he was accustomed to. The restaurant was just far too noisy. He was far too calm.

"Great. Here. Follow me, please," the waitress said, scattering menus together and power walking to the back. A busboy, of equal levels of stress, threw the soiled plates in and wiped down with a plausibly dirty cloth.

"At least it's not *as* loud back here," she giggled.

"What are you hungry for?"

"You still don't know my name, do you?"

Jeff felt a prick in his lower back. He was unsure if it was a residual side effect of his copulation, or he was found guilty of her assumption. With a gulp of the water that was innocuously placed there, he took a big gulp.

"No."

"Samantha."

"Got ya. I have a thing for unisex names."

Samantha sputtered.

"What the hell do you—"

"Sam. Duh." He finally smiled.

"You're a goof," she said, kicking his shin. The waitress returned.

"You two are cute together! Here on finals week, grabbing some grub before you 'hit the books'?" She attempted to fit in, despite her name tag displaying a '25 year' sticker on it.

"Yes. That's *exactly* what we are going to do," Samantha said, coyly. "I'll go with a short stack. Extra butter, please."

"What she's having, but extra jam. Strawberry. Also, can I get a side of home fries? For the table."

"That was easy!" She looked at Jeff. "How about an energy drink? You sure look like you need a pick-me-up?"

"I'll pass, thanks. Just water."

The waitress grinned, flaunting a few perfectly white teeth.

"You know, all that butter will go right to your thighs," Jeff said, bitterly.

Samantha slapped her exposed thigh.

"Yes, cause that's *exactly* what these bones need!"

Jeff smirked at her sardonic remark.

"Good."

They continued with small talk until their food arrived. More people entered the diner. It was only 10:30.

"Guess everyone wants to study for once. Good riddance." Jeff said.

"Oh, you are just a curmudgeon!" Samantha said, plowing into her pancakes in a voracious, uncouth manner.

"Jeez, woman. You sure—"

"Ah. Say it with me. Sa-man…"

"…tha. Ok, Samantha."

"You need to learn some manners, Jeffrey," She cut some pancakes and the knife slid along the ceramic with a screech. "Keep me around long enough, I'll turn you straight."

Jeff laughed. "Sure!"

He picked up some shredded home fries.

"So, *Samantha*. You are graduating this term, correct?"

"Yes, fucking *finally!* I've just about had it with Stone Pony and some of these professors. I swear some of these men are downright misogynists, talking down vicariously through their critiques. Plus, the editing is boring me. Nothing good, well, aside from your genius."

"Where is home for you?"

"Oh, well I'm from Colorado. Plan on moving back. No jobs lined up around here, so I may just have to look around."

Jeff hunched forward, as to keep a confidential ear about.

"Look. I need you for something. I only told one other person about this, but I think we can make something happen."

She leaned in, very close. She pecked his lips. Jeff tasted the butter.

"Tell me."

"I want to start a publishing company. I'm talking *way* more than a journal. Yes, it will be a staple in the company, but there is much more. Kind of like if Ferlinghetti fucked Virginia Woolf, but better! Ha-ha, this is only the beginning of it really and I have been up for many days at a time to gather—"

"Babe! You're going off the rails. Remember what I told you in your room: pace yourself."

Jeff's faced blushed the same hue as the strawberry jam on his pancakes.

"So, you want to make a publishing company. One that is both literary and...?"

"Professional," Jeff stated. "I want to bring in writers that only Stone Pony could dream of publishing. They try too hard to compete with Iowa; it's trite and elementary. I will give them—Iowa, that is—a run for their money in time."

Samantha was engrossed in his valiant idea she almost forgot the ability to speak.

"That's so cool!" she cried. "Hold on let me grab another bite before I start drooling over it."

"I just need a partner to be there for a second opinion. For curation. For marketeering. I would ask my friend, Max—-or so I believed was my friend—but I have no idea what he is going to do. I live in New Mexico, so not too far from you.

"So, you're insinuating we move in together?"

"In short, yes. But, we will be moving in together elsewhere."

"Like?"

"California."

"Ooh!" She said, exuberantly. "I always wanted to go to Los Angeles."

"That's where I want to go. Best place there is for exposure. Are you in? I want to make it official."

"And how?" She carried on the antics. "You already fucked me like you left prison."

"I am a man of merit, but you should know what I like already," Jeff said, seductively. He drew her by the t-shirt she was wearing until she was in lethal range. She nibbled on his earlobe, coincidentally at the same time the waitress returned.

"Well, I guess I'll leave you two whippersnappers be for a few more minutes," her face became visibly distraught; that of long lust. The couple paid her no mind. "Still...got some bites left."

Samantha exhaled.

"You got yourself a promise."

Nine

River Chang felt pretty good with his rockstar status assured in the graduate program at Texas Tech. He was the talk of the MFA program and with a new chapbook, *Visions in Red Sky,* his writing career was thriving. Despite his success, there was an impedance that kept popping up on his blog, somebody had been trolling every time he posted a poem. It didn't bother him at first, but now it seemed the troll delighted in criticizing every post he made. Chang took pride in his blog, it was a way for communicating with his readers and posting his work for his thousands of followers. Chang had tried to block the annoying commenter, however, it seemed every time he did a new user would just take its place.

The whole thing seemed preposterous but the sad thing was that many of his readers were agreeing with the anonymous. River had written another controversial poem entitled, "Hate and Buddy Holly": a brutal attack against West Texas. The East Coast crowd delighted in River's poem, calling it a genius attack on the backward thinking of the ignorant common people in places like Texas. To combat the disdain, Chang rallied the thinktanks and poets in the liberal capital of Austin and its motto, 'Keep Austin Weird'. They embraced the progressive thinking River so often put in his poetry. Immediately following. It was a tit for tat battle: "Hate and Buddy Holly" being published in the liberal magazine, *Left Feed* while "Faux News and Sexual Waste" was published in the even more influential conservative magazine, *Right Wing Nutjob*.

River knew that the poem was a direct response and attack on his essay and though it burned him up inside, River admired the writing by some poet named Maurice Wilson. Chang did a Google search of such and the only thing that turned up was the poem in *Right Wing Nutjob*. He started to piece things together. There wasn't any proof of course, but could this Maurice be the troll that lambasted him on his blog?

***

Max rubbed his eyes and sat up in bed. He staggered to his writing desk and turned on his laptop. He delighted in knowing his poem "Faux News and Sexual Waste" had become the talk of local conservatives and the fact that some commenter said his poem was a direct response to a poem by River Chang. Max bellowed in laughter. *Check.* Max had single-handedly started a 'poetry war' and soon it would be the talk of the online poetic community. Max hated community, much less a poetry one that existed in cyberspace. Max thought as he turned on his smartphone and logged onto his Glanceagram account.

"Holy shit!" Max screamed. He had gained almost six hundred thousand followers overnight and then realized his 'she poem' must have been reposted by Karen Kramer. Max immediately went to Karen's page and then he saw it. "I love this by @tyleryoung" Karen had posted his poem!

"Oh, what moronic sheep. Her mass following actually thinks "She is she" is the pinnacle of literature." This was the game changer that Max had been waiting for, and now he was more popular than all the 'she poets' with one post. All it took was something so moronically simple. Max wanted to tell Jeff as soon as possible, but something told him to wait. His profile was booming, with nothing but airheaded comments like 'Wow' and 'Truth'. Nothing of substance, but it was a quick rush of joy to what he saw as a joke.

"What morons. I've tapped into a gold mine."

Max put his phone down and logged onto his school email. There were several from Dean Waters and his professors, saying he was in danger of failing for the semester, due to missed tests and lack of attendance. Dean Waters threatened to toss out his application to the MFA program if Max did not contact him immediately. What really made Max laugh, is that Dean Waters said he had evidence that Max had committed academic fraud, which meant expulsion from the university.

"That will be the least of this pissant's concerns."

Max had made up his mind, he wasn't going back to class and Texas Tech could kiss his ass. He was paid up for room and board through the end of the semester, and that gave him enough time to unleash what Max had deemed, 'The Reckoning'. In addition to all the social media excitement of the morning, Max noticed that Julie had texted him over fifty times.

"I can't deal with this. What does she want from me? Another ol' session of the in and out?" Max ignored most of the messages but one simply said,

I'm late

Max shuttered to think what that might mean. His darkest fear came over him. Did he impregnate Julie? This was the last thing he needed, just when the world seemed to be his oyster.

Ten

Professor Greene sat in his office completely unaware that he was about to be fired by Dean Waters. Waters would call it a sabbatical, but the reality is he never wanted Greene to set foot on campus again. Sure, there would a nice severance package, but if Waters had his way, Greene would never teach again at the university level. Greene worked for years trying to be a distinguished poet, releasing numerous chapbooks with little recognition or fanfare. He even failed to get into some of the more prestigious literary magazines, and to make matters worse, a few students that he instructed had bested him. Namely River Chang and Max Wilson. Greene confided to Anderson that he believed Max was writing other students' papers in his class but without real proof, Greene's accusation seemed a lost cause.

What seemed even more preposterous, is that the Julie was basking in her newfound celebrity in the English Department. Greene knew Julie was a mediocre writer at best, and not capable of penning the "Malthusian Essay" that she was taking credit for. Was Max Wilson behind this deception? Greene pondered these things when his desk phone rang.

"This is Professor Greene."

"Greene, what the hell are you doing?" Dean Waters said with a tinge of anger in his voice.

"Just grading a few essays."

"You find any more genius from Ms. Pinner?" Waters knew that even if Greene's inclination was correct, and this Max Wilson did write Julie's paper, it meant nothing. He would keep her around by pulling a few strings. She was the Golden Girl, and Water's late-night sensation.

"I haven't graded anything else from Ms. Pinner, but now that you mention it, there is an issue. I believe someone else may have written the paper. I don't have actual proof but it's possible Max Wilson wrote it. A few of the students mentioned that Max is in a relationship with Ms. Pinner. When comparing his and this latest one, I've noticed the same syntax, similar diction, and—"

"That's horseshit and you know it, Greene. I had the pleasure of talking with Julie as you know, and let me tell you. what a brilliant woman and writer she is. In fact, I already offered an acceptance into the MFA program when she's completed her undergraduate studies."

"You did? I strongly disagree as Ms. Pinner is a lackluster student, and nothing she's written is even close to the "Malthusian essay" that she supposedly wrote. Believe me, I don't think that she could have written the paper."

"Shut up, Greene! That's a blasphemous accusation, and I believe Ms. Pinner told me the real reason you have gotten such nonsensical ideas in your head, is the fact being, your teaching isn't up to par with your students' needs as she confided to me."

"That's a very subjective statement. As you know, my evaluations have been sturdy for the past four academic years and—"

"The real reason that I called is that your sabbatical starts next week. I have taken care of everything and the board approved it. You simply need to clean out your office and leave, and don't worry I have a student ready to take over your class."

"But...next week? Takeover, *my* class? A student...who the hell is it?" Greene was incensed at the odd news.

"It's not a termination, but a permanent sabbatical, and don't worry you'll get a nice going-away check. By the way, if you must know who is filling your shoes, it's the Golden Boy. Chang will do an excellent job educating your former students. Have a good day Professor...I mean...Mr. Greene."

Waters slammed the phone causing a loud thud in Greene's ear.

Greene wheezed, causing his face to turn blood red. "He can't get away with this, that son of a bitch." He opened his email and fired off a series of messages to the Board of Regents about Waters. Perhaps, Greene could sue the university, but then it all came crashing down on him. "Those fuckers and their eminent domain." Greene threw a textbook across the room, causing a small dent in the drywall. He sank down in his chair, nearly weeping. The end never really comes until it does.

***

The thorn in Texas Tech University's side was the Barry Motel. The motel sat across the street from the school and it was a hotbed for winos, junkies, and whores. The university tried to purge it by buying the land around it for future storefronts. They even tried a buyout, but the owners were not biting. Max loved the motel. The first thing he did when he visited Tech for Freshman Orientation was to check in since it gave him nostalgia from when his family would travel. His dad thought these rundown motels were ideal for sharing the gospel with the dregs of society. They never did convert anybody, but his father said that only God could change a heart, and all they had to do was plant the seed.

The old man sat behind the desk. Max remembered him from his previous visit.

"Mr. Lester. Not sure if you remember me, I'm Max Wilson. I met you several years ago."

"Max you back!" Ray Lester jumped up to his feet when he saw his friend enter through the front door.

"How things been?" Max asked.

"Awful. We got no customers, things been slow. How things go for you?"

"Almost done with my classes…" Max spotted a tall African-American man walk through the front door. The man had on a blond wig and red lipstick and he was wearing a dress.

"Oh, Patricia, this is Max," Lester said, introducing the pair.

"I haven't." Max extended his hand.

"Nice to meet you Max, we sure done heard about you." Patricia's tenor voice perturbed him, but nonetheless, seemed like a nice woman.

"Hopefully good things."

"I got to be getting across town but I see you later. I didn't forget your double meat burger." Patricia handed Lester a greasy sack and said goodbye.

"She sure is a nice lady, well you know she ain't really a lady."

"I figured that you know you could upgrade some things around here."

"Upgrade? What you mean Max?"

"I mean you need some technology, get some computers with internet for your records and some security cameras."

"That sound fancy, what you mean internet?"

"The world wide web, you'll love it. The cameras will help you keep an eye on things."

"Leroy, keep an eye out. Sometimes he ain't around though. That sound like it cost a lot. We ain't got money to be throwing 'round."

"I have plenty of money. It won't take me long to get it set up."

"Really? That sound mighty good."

"You say mighty good a lot," Max laughed.

"That mighty good, I don't know how to thank you. I mean you busy over there being a scholar at the school when you be back with the fancy internet?"

"Soon, I'll go buy the equipment and set it up."

"Mighty good."

"One more thing, you ever have customers from the university?"

"You mean the school?"

"Can you think of anyone? I want you to think."

"Let's see." Lester scratched his head and thought. "Now that I think about it, this fat man come in not long ago. I never know he from the school, but Leroy says he saw him come over. The man dressed fancy in a suit, and what not. I think his name Water. He requested one of the girls and got a room. Come to think of it, he get room 117. Yeah, that's it, he come before and always get that room. It way in the back."

"It's a good idea to put a security camera in that room, so he doesn't cheat you out of money."

"You right, that sound mighty good." Lester smiled thinking Max sure smart.

"I'll put a camera in that room."

"Mighty good, matter fact he do seem cheap."

"I'll be back in a few days with the gear."

***

"What you say, Max?" Lester stood up when he saw Max walk into his motel.

"Doing good, how's the new gear working for you?"

"It sure fancy, I think everything mighty good. Have a little problem with mine here at my desk."

"Let me look at it. Did you turn it on?"

"What you say, Max?"

Max pushed the power button and it came on.

"There it go." Lester's eyes lit up when he saw the screen come one. "Sure is fancy, mighty good," Lester said.

"Just hit that button, if you want to turn it on."

"How you turn it off?"

"Hit the button."

"What button?"

"The same one."

"Mighty good; you a whiz at computer. How everything going over at da school?"

"Studying hard, where are the other computers?"

"Leroy took 'em to the pawn shop, say he got top dollar."

"Why'd he do that?"

"Say they too flashy."

Max sighed, knowing that his money literally went in and out.

"I need you to do something for me. I put that camera in room one seventeen. It's on twenty-four hours a day."

"That almost all day. What you need Max?"

"When that fat guy comes over from across the street, make sure he gets room one seventeen."

"He always do, I got some girls back. I make sure he get the nicest looking one. I tell Suzie to go home if she show up."

"How is Suzie?"

"She good, getting too many miles though. May need to let her go."

"Ah, that's a shame," Max lied. "Here's my cell phone number, I want you to call me after the fat man visits."

"I sure will."

"How is Patricia?" Max asked.

"She good. She stay with her mom over in Slaton for the weekend."

"One more thing. The university has a big banquet in May, and I got tickets for you, Patricia, Suzie, and Leroy."

"What they do at the banquet?"

"Just eat, drink, and read poetry."

"That sound fun. We be there. I won't lose the tickets; put them in a safe place."

"Don't forget to call me after the fat man visits."

"I won't forget, thank you, Max. It sure mean a lot to us. You like part 'a family now."

"You're welcome." Max laughed to himself, thinking about Lester and the gang showing up at the English Department's end of the year party.

"I think you told me that last time. Things been good around here?"

"I'll see ya around," Max said, departing with a wave. As he was exiting, he saw a curmudgeon leaning against the wall with a large bottle wrapped in a brown bag.

"Hi there," the man said.

"Hi."

"Want some of this?"

"I'm good," Max said, disdainfully.

"Reckon you had a good time in there?"

"Nah, was just visiting the old man Lester."

"Oh, you say? I'm Leroy."

"What did you say?" Max could hardly understand him.

"Leroy. I'm the security."

"Great to hear it, pal," Max said. "Did you guys get new cameras and stuff?"

"Yeah, some young buck did for us. I got rid of most. Too damn bright and flashy."

Eleven

Jeff's only part-time job was at a small bookstore off-campus, Books-A-Thousand. He didn't like to tell anyone, since everytime he was on the clock, he felt that at least one undercover FBI agent visited. They sold the typical bestsellers and classic literature, but there was also a section that hosted many indie books: Mexican-American protest poems, neo-communist, and other radical works lined a small corner shelf. He would typically get five customers that genuinely needed help finding a book, and that was particularly in that small section. "It's for a class." "I'm a proletariat, too." "Can you direct me to a book in, and excuse me if I'm saying this wrong: Rastafarianism?" were typical questions he would get. Most of the time though, he would sit on the worn out cushioned stool, swirling a chai tea from the local coffee roaster. He'd rather watch the ice melt than seeing shelves of the books stand untouched by the masses.

It was easy to work nonetheless. Cashiering, stocking books that weighed 5 pounds or less and counting money at night. Nothing difficult. He would indulge in the texts that Texas Tech wasn't privy on, especially when he would grow weary of literature and wanted a more sociological aspect or verify that Roe v. Wade was indeed not a boxing match. The owner was insouciant and smoked many cigarettes on his breaks. If anything, Jeff could convince that he spent a few bucks on a pack of smokes, and not into Jeff's pocket. It did not matter for he was about to be finished with it completely.

One night, as Jeff was counting the money, he noticed a large mass of people flock to a competing bookstore, Barney & Jules, for a book signing. It took Jeff's customers away. He took a moment to gaze out the window, propping his elbows on the sill. Droves of people, varying from youth to elderly, entered the bookstore, which was light fairly well, to see another bloated author with a six-figure advance. He would sit there, judging them, seeing novels in their hands with a holographic logo on the spine. He loathed the commercialization of it all, desperately willing for something better to capture the attention of the masses.

He scoured the shelves for a more prominent book, one that was both contemporary and contained a prominent purpose. He looked and looked. Nothing. He checked the back corner shelf, thinking that the best socialist text since sliced Marx wasn't the best option to be parading around the streets of a right-wing locale. Fearing that he was going to miss the crowd, he grasped a book from the bestseller list and darted outside. He stood under a streetlamp, hoisting the book up high.

"Fellow citizens of the Lone Star State! May I have your attention! For years, you all have been led astray by the capitalistic structures of publishing. Alas, I have a solution for you all. Here, in my hands, is a tome of great proportions. One that stimulates the mind and draws critical social commentary to all who dare read it!"

Some people looked at his scraggly hair overtop of a red flannel and laughed. His image and performance surely matched.

"Dude, you fucking suck!" a lone voice emitted. Jeff lost them before he even had them.

"And...the best part...you can pay what you want. That's right, *pay whatever.* Hell, take a book from there and use it as store credit. We don't price gouge a single—"

"Boo, go away, you hobo!"

"Mommy! That man scares me..."

Jeff continued to make a fool of himself, only attracting a few passersby's to carelessly glance at his store, then flee. A single Barney & Jules employee waded through the crowd and whistled. Jeff paused, lowering the book.

"Excuse me, sir. We've been getting complaints. Please stop or we will call the police."

"Oh yeah? This is our marketing routine...every...*other* Tuesday! My manager will not enjoy hearing this." Jeff snickered.

"Dialing…" the woman said, which called Jeff's bluff. He stomped inside, letting the rickety door bid adieu to the crowd. Inside, a single customer was at the counter. Jeff sat the book down and assumed his deflated position.

"Find everything you needed, sir?"

"Uh, yes, thank you." The man looked over at the book Jeff had. "Oh, him? Not the best type of book to be parading around here, but hey, I watched and heard you. Can I give you…" he rummaged through his pocket. "…three dollars and…twenty-eight cents?"

Jeff took a glimpse at the book: It was River Chang! Out of all the bestsellers, that was the one he blindly chose.

"Oh, *that* guy. I'll take pennies for it."

"Deal. I hear he goes to school right down the road. Be nice to see a liberal's perspective in this day and age." The man paid the change, along with a twenty for the others books and left. He carried them under his arms, with Chang's beaming smile glaring back at Jeff from the back cover.

"Didn't Max say something about him before? Whatever, it's closing time," Jeff said as he flicked the 'OPEN 'sign off for the third to last time.

Twelve

Max stared at his phone in the darkness. He saw the notification light illuminate his private poetry dungeon; things had spiraled out of control on his Glanceagram page. His last poem simply read, "she loves", and it amassed over fifty-thousand likes. Max was receiving direct messages from women almost non-stop and many asked if he had a book for sale and if he was single. This gave Max an idea of releasing a book of these particular poems. He could use it as his days at Texas Tech were numbered, with hardly any kind of career in sight, and if anything, his decision to drop out gave him relief. Independence from the daily struggles. Max had grown tired of academia, and if need be, he could always go back to school to finish his degree, just not here. Absolutely not. What good is a degree in English anyways especially if you hate it so?

An ensuing flurry of *blips* forced him to check his phone. The blinking light reminded him of a poem that he saw on Glanceagram by another popular she poet, it read: "she is my moon in my darkness". It was horrible, but still thousands of likes. Max didn't dwell on it too long.

I'm pregnant

The text from Julie sent a shockwave through Max's body and he felt his bowels shake.

"That lusty wench," Max groaned.

The whole night of the supposed conception must've been a trick. She invited him over to write the research paper, as a front for fertilization. His response was impulsive, to say the least:

Deal with it

The words were cold-blooded, but Max felt St. Augustine within his soul. He wasn't ready to be a father, and a future with Julie was out of the question. He put it out of his mind because he believed Julie was lying.

"That evil strumpet, she probably got impregnated by River Chang," Max said, reassuring himself. "All the attention she's been giving the English department…there's no doubt."

It seemed all Julie did was blab about Chang and the greatness of his 'poetry'. The more Max thought about his book idea, the more it appealed to him. He could publish the book himself if he could man the wheel and do it; he despised the cop-out of self-publishing. The only question that remained was: who would publish crap like this? It all sounded trite and uninteresting. He went to the kitchen for a glass of water.

Returning, Max sat on the edge of his bed and turned his flashlight on. He eyed the treatise sitting on the desk. It would be the last thing to mail as he walked away from Texas Tech forever. He'd drop it in the mailbox, and then envision Lisa Polk getting it and slowly reading each line in utter disgust. The treatise wasn't only his masterpiece, it was a harangue against putrid literature and the snobs that enabled it. Maybe the feedback he was destined to receive from it would boost his rise to the top? No, it was not the time to unleash the beast. He needed yet another project, one that had a more physical impact. He already planted the seed at the Barry Motel, but there was still puzzle pieces that were missing.

He had limited amount of time left on campus, barring any potential expulsion. He needed to come up with a plan to complete his utter destruction of the Texas Tech English Department. Max's neurons began firing at a rapid pace as he grabbed a pen and paper, he penned "The Great Escape." It was a comprehensive list that would cover all the bases in one fell swoop. The dunces in their ivory towers would never see it coming, and elitist 'lit clubs' on campus would have their pious egos ruined. How many times had Max submitted to Stone Pony? No response. Not even a formal rejection letter, which every writer worth their salt knew as a common courtesy.

If anything, Max had surpassed the Golden Boy in literary 'street cred' but yet, even his own university completely ignored him. Now, Dean Waters and the faculty would celebrate Chang's coronation at the end of the year awards banquet. There was a rumor being that even Julie herself would give one of the keynote speeches in front of the graduate school, which seemed ludicrous. As Max suspected, the blame was being shifted on him—as it should after all—and that alone called for his ultimate revenge. But revenge didn't seem like to proper name, reckoning seemed more appropriate for the hell that was about to be unleashed.

"The Great Escape"

I. The Strumpet of Lubbock

II. Operation Rotten Egg

III. Role the Footage

IV. Tip of the Hat

***

Julie plummeted into a paranoiac state. She possessed a newfound anxiety every time she mingled with her peers, even some professors. She also was wary of Dean Water's intentions. Her intuition suspected that he was up to lewdness. And now, her latest stint with Max was at a head. She lied to him about being pregnant. Julie couldn't stand that Max had been ignoring her, but in a way, she felt an unquenchable attraction to him. She also felt remorse, knowing that such a careless request caused her much success and him a possibly bleak future, at least at Texas Tech. As finals approached, she could see the end in sight, yet had to cut a few cords away to get there.

Julie studied her notes when her phone vibrated. She read the text from Max and trembled. How could he feel that way? Didn't he love her? What about their future together? It was then that she nearly broke down. She flung her notebook and everything on the desk and yelled so loud that not even Max's most snide remark could quell. She might never speak to Max again and Waters wouldn't take no for an answer. She calmed herself by drinking a glass of water and masturbating. If Max didn't want her, at least she knew her worth, and that speech was going to be one for the ages.

Thirteen

Graduation day arrived for the seniors early. Doe-eyed and anxious young adults were scattered around the grounds of the stadium like fire ants upon the grass. Their black, scarlet, and white robes shimmered in the hot Texas spring. Jeff, stoic in demeanor, walked with Samantha hand-in-hand. She was ecstatic at the outlandish presentation, pulling and tugging at his hand going every which way, occasionally dropping into a picture with friends. This event meant more to her than Jeff could even comprehend; it took some heavy convincing to even get him to attend. All he cared about was his nurtured plan. It was his one true love. He rationalized in his head: *"If I can make it through a couple hours of this frivolous bullshit, then time is all mine."*

"Jeffy! Smile, dammit. This is a special moment for all of us."

He scoffed. "I'll think about it."

"Sourpuss", she said, nudging him in the ribs. "C'mon, let's go sit down."

The couple grabbed their name cards and sat in the cramped seating. He paid no mind; the heat made Jeff undo his tie a bit. Samantha was bantering with some classmates from Stone Pony behind them. Jeff did pay mind to this conversation.

"...he has a wonderful idea. Something about a lit mag..."

"Talk about endearing. This damn woman."

As almost on cue, the decorum began. The chancellor, followed by prominent faculty in their respective garbs strode onto the stage.

"They look like that one guy from Pocahontas. I'm sure some are racist too."

Chancellor Rails took the podium, yet he seemed anxious as if someone was watching him from a distance, or even a sniper scope. His chagrin was easily deciphered by Jeff.

"What a prick. Just talk already"

"It is said that with age, comes inherited wisdom, be it from your peers' own introspection or that of the muses that you research, that you model your own life off—"

Jeff peered over to Samantha, who was fully committed to his speech; so was the vast herd of his collegiate sheep. Jeff groaned softly, which warranted a quick jab in the rib by her elbow. He behaved.

The rows of students were being ushered to take the stage. Samantha's face exuberated pride while Jeff's was sullen; quite a Manichean performance to show off to Rails. Before he knew it, he was watching his girlfriend obtain her degree and hearing the pronunciation of his first name being called. It sounded like a reactionary response to when someone bumps into you at a grocery store. "JEF-free". Where the fuck was the third syllable? His very name had the connotation of the annoyed, the perturbed. Either way, he slogged across the stage to eventually receive his tens of thousands in paper form by a cuck of a man—Max told him of some rumors prior to their estrangement—who received his 7-inch long beard and disconsolate eyes with a look of empathy and equity. Jeff walked off the stage with an unfamiliar tingling in his spine. Despite his rigid demeanor, his innards were ablaze with aspiration. He swore he had a complex, but his ill-tempered self was absolved by Samantha's plump lips upon his cheek.

He was now a college graduate, and his master plan was but minutes away from blossoming into the pit of his chest. The ceremony ended and he transformed in front of the cameras of Samantha's father and step-mother; he wanted to leave a good first impression. All the while, he looked outward, beyond the stadium extents, and into the horizon and the heat radiating off the clay and asphalt around Lubbock, and the aspirations and passion radiating off the gowns of his ecstatic peers. His parents never made the trip to see him graduate.

***

Max watched the stadium from the rooftop of Bledsoe Hall with a six pack and a pan pizza. He was seated in a lawn chair with shades on, viewing his Glanceagram account had almost a million followers. He cranked out multiple poems of universal simplicity, burping after each one.

"This…this is the life." He said, hearing the echoes of his graduating peers, hardly caring about his lapse. Max believed that his hoodwinking of the pseudo-virtual writing community was nothing short of pure genius. But could Max use his facade to sell his *real* books? It certainly was worth a try. Max added a link to his Shamazon page with some of his previously published chapbooks. It was now that his social media 'experiment' began. Would these morons buy his real book even though it was published under Max Wilson and not the infamous Tyler Young?

Max had won a chapbook contest with a small press in upstate New York, but like most things requiring talent, his achievement was ignored. The publishing game had changed and although Max wanted a reputable publisher for his satirical 'she-poem' book, he knew with time, things would come together, maybe teach a lesson or two about writing along the way. The future was looking as crisp as the sky he saw.

"Oh, what genius."

He found an image of for his forthcoming chapbook, *Dirty Panties and Pelagius*, then posted it on his account, making sure to write a caption stating it was his first ever book. 'Coming so soon, my loves'.

Max called Paul Garrett the publisher of his chapbooks in Houston to let him know to check for any new sales.

"New sales? We sold one book in the last six months and that was your mother," Paul said. He chuckled a bit, as the asshole he was.

"Don't remind me, but listen, I'm trying something new; an experiment if you will, so just giving you a heads up to look for more sales."

"Sounds interesting, I will check and you can log in to our sales account as well remember? Maybe we will get two or three sales a month. You never know."

Max knew he wasn't taking the bait.

"You're going to be surprised my friend just wait and see. Oh, one other thing I forgot the password.

"Really? It's RollingRock69, case sensitive."

"Oh yeah, maybe we should change that."

"No. That *is* you. We will have to seek sponsorship one day. Everything else going well?' Paul wanted to be friendly now.

"I can't begin to tell you everything now. Sitting here watching a graduation, but I will say expect cash to be rolling in."

"Wait, I thought you were graduating?"

"Plans changed. I had an epiphany."

"Which is?"

"This new chapbook."

"I don't know Max, nobody gets the title of your book. I mean, dirty panties and Pelagius? I've been out of school for a while and I had to look this old fool up. And the book is mainly a collection of academic and satirical rants that few comprehend. I love you, man, but your mind is too brilliant for this press. Wish I could get you overseas…"

"Relax! The title was the first thing that came to me. It will be perfect, trust me."

"Ok. I'll hold you to it. Have a good rest of the day."

Max hung up and set another empty bottle in the holder. This time, there would be no failure. The only thing being, there was exactly two weeks before he had to move off campus. The end of the year awards banquet was coming close and the ghost of St. Augustine would be there to crash the party.

Fourteen

Dean Waters, who watched the ceremony from his cozy office, lit a cigar. He needed to contact Julie and Chang about the event, but his carnal desires wanted something else. They both had brought literary integrity to the department, which equated to a larger budget and student enrollment next year. After dragging the cigar halfway, he extinguished it and wrote the email.

To my dearest students, Julie and River,

Thursday, we will begin preparing for the banquet. Regardless if you've chosen to walk today, you will be given even higher honors on this day. It is optional, but your academic futures would greatly benefit from it. We have reps from Barney & Jules, Cornell University, and The Bluffington Bias are scheduled to attend and are *very* excited to meet you both. Hope to see you there...

—Dean Waters

Waters smiled as he clicked 'Send'. His mind fantasized as to what Julie might wear.

"A tight, little, black dress I hope," he said, aloud. His forehead began perspiring.

Waters caught word that Max Wilson had possibly dropped out; no one had seen him in weeks, both in class and around campus. He had no worries about the academic fraud anymore, for the alleged perpetrator was out of his hair and plans would continue as planned. If he were to rear his disgusting head, he would certainly seek legal matters to crush his scheme. The other pleasantry was the removal of Professor Greene from his dream of finishing out his career at Texas Tech.

"He'll never get another job and what Greene deserves is to be on a cargo boat to Hong Kong," Waters muttered. Waters had a chance to leave the 'armpit of academia' in just one academic year. Retirement was in sight and Lubbock would be in his rearview mirror. It reminded him of the song by John Davis, "Happiness is Lubbock, Texas in the Past". It had always been one of the Waters' favorites. He opened his laptop and unzipped his fly. Things were going to be perfect for his pupils' coronation, he could sense it.

***

Max threw away everything in his dorm room. Nobody seemed to care that he dropped out of his classes. He was certain the English department rejoiced in his absence. With two weeks left before school closed for the summer, he was too engorged on his master plan.

Max's 'Glanceagram' page exploded, amassing almost two million followers. Max even came up with a proper term for this style of two lined gibberish: pop-poetry. It was spreading like wildfire on the internet. The best thing about it was he was selling more books than ever. With weekly sales updates from Garrett, the press was no longer in the red, and he was finally getting more cash in his pocket. Max still didn't mail the treatise though. He stared at the oversized envelope wondering if getting revenge at *WANK* was even necessary. He thought that maybe they found new targets to chastise, but at the same time, he wanted things to be up-close and personal. More than likely, he was too busy plotting "The Great Escape" to even care. He pushed it to the corner and his phone rang.

"Max, you devil!" Paul Garrett said. "You really pulled through."

"Told ya," Max said. 99% of the time when I say so, it happens."

"These sales are phenomenal. You and this Glanceagram…pure genius! Our suppliers can't even keep up with the demand. We'll need to chop down an entire forest."

"Good, let's keep it flowing. I need a good vacation. Greece, I suppose."

"Consider it done. I got to go…paper just arrived."

Max was elated to hear the good news. He was certain literary sects from all over the world were taking in his chapbook, let alone hundreds of thousands of blithe readers. He knew his mind and ruse were working together and that soon Chang would be dethroned from the NYT's best-seller list. Ironically, there was not a bigger elitist than Max himself, tinged with a hint of narcissism that would make Caligula blush.

"Oh, what horseshit is this," Max said as he reached into his small refrigerator to grab another Rolling Rock; the last bottle was half drunk. He took a giant swig, feeling the golden lager slide down his throat and for a moment he felt a sense of peace. He thought more about phase one, 'The Strumpet of Lubbock' had become the scam of the department and watching horny Dean Waters try mercilessly to get in Julie's pants. It was a comic delight. He lobbed the empty bottle into the trash like he was one of the basketball team. He would clearly be the center with a terrible jump shot since the bottle clinked the edge and bounced onto the carpet.

Max searched for the Malthusian research paper. He composed a new email and attached it. He was certain that Chancellor Rails would be interested in this fiasco. Max took a deep breath and leaned back in his chair, rereading the entire message.

Chancellor Rails,

It is with deep regret that I committed academic fraud for using a research paper that I didn't write. I borrowed the paper and put my name on it, not thinking of the consequences of my deceit. I turned the paper into Professor Greene and received an 'A', but it's with a heavy heart that another student 'River Chang' deserves credit for the paper. It isn't my intention to bring him into this matter, but we both deserve whatever punishment you deem appropriate. I'm sorry for dishonoring the integrity of Texas Tech University.

Sincerely,

Julie Pinner

Max hit the send button and logged off Julie's account. He wiped his sweating brow and sighed. 'The Strumpet of Lubbock' was completed.

"Hell, hath no fury," he muttered.

Fifteen

Post graduate life was upon Jeff, yet for once, he was not alone. Samantha rode shotgun in his diesel Volvo 240 wagon, smoking a blunt, and donning tattered jeans and a v-cut Slayer t-shirt. Jeff, wearing a rolled-up flannel, slicked back hair, and an old pair of Ray-Cans he picked up at a thrift store. The arid desert air intermingled with the diesel exhaust. Their flippant attitude to college was that of the Beats, except that Jeff had no regard for the counterculture or liberal ideologies. He was methodical. He was precise. He had dozens of pages of notes scribbled into an old pad. He was the architect of the grandest facade that would easily overthrow Stone Pony.

"Hey babe, have you heard of this Glanceagram app? It looks pretty cool!" Samantha said, carelessly scrolling on her iPhone.

"I don't have the time for something like that."

"Oh, these models are cute. They have makeup tutorials and such. Hey! There are celebrities on here. Karen Kramer, ugh. I wish I could be like her."

"Why must you compare yourself to these blithe people, running around causing amuck on the internet."

"Oh! She posted a picture of some poem on here."

"What does it say?"

"Hmm. 'I once tried to love, but the whiskey bottle stole my heart first and never gave it up.' Over 20,000 likes, now that's impressive—"

"Whatever the fuck that was, sounded like a 9th grader finding his old man's liquor cabinet."

"...and over two hundred comments. People love this guy, well, at least I assume that's who it is."

"Name?"

"H.R. Snake. Let me check."

Samantha browsed the profile of this alleged poet. He was a bearded man, like Jeff, but donned a man-bun, rounded sunglasses, and wore designer "OBEY" t-shirt on, staring pretentiously into the ether. A grassy knoll backgrounded him. The picture in its entirety was enshrouded in a grayscale filter. His follower count was through the roof. All his posts fit exactly within the allotted space a cell phone screen could allow.

"Does it say where he has been previously published?"

"No," she said. "His biography says: 'Moon-child of the Nebraskan fields. Bookie. Amazonian poetic genius' and also a few emojis."

Jeff bellowed a hearty laugh.

"So. You're telling me this crackpot has *no* literary publications but is amassing hundreds of thousands of people with his trite, heavily cliched work?"

"That's exactly what I'm saying. It isn't the *best* work per say, but it draws a crowd."

Jeff pinned the gas pedal down. The RPM's whirred, forcing more air into the cabin. Samantha's joint flew out of her outstretched arm.

"I wasn't done with that, Jeff. Slow the fuck down!"

"This is why I don't dabble in this age of social media. It's far from social, it's narcissistic and frivolous. I studied T.S. Eliot, Pound, Yeats, and Longfellow in my day, and they would dismiss this bastard poetry in one sentence. Red Wheelbarrow has more substance than all this guy's page."

"You are correct, Jeff. However, if you want to have a presence in the 21st century, social media is the way to go. Do you expect people to read the work of an ant in an anthill? Your work is wonderful, babe. Cerebral and critical. But remember the audiences you want to bring in to your journal. Obviously, you want the dedication and affirmation of the affluent, but what about the layman? If anything, you should consider having a guy, or woman, like this Snake as your, well, poster child. At least until you get going."

Jeff remained silent, lost in his thoughts. He slowed down and began tapping the steering wheel with his left hand. A mystic drumbeat filled the cabin, along with the clunky air conditioning. Samantha gripped the panic handle. She was worried his neurotic version was rebirthing.

"Hey, uh, Jeff? Babe? I didn't mean anything—"

"You know what?" he said. "That is the most ingenious thing you've said."

She laughed with apprehension. "Really? I didn't think that was—"

"Sign me up for an account. This wasn't in my original plans, mostly because I hate marketing crap, but I can tweak some components to make this work."

"I know this means so much to you," she said, staring attentively at her phone.

"I'm elated! I never would've thought that this Glanceagram would be a harbor of such manipulation, um, I mean, *exposure,* yes."

"What?"

"Exposure."

"Oh, I got ya." She paused. "Babe, I need a username. Do you just want to use the name of the journal? For now?"

"Certainly. Name this account: Smokey J Quarterly. Oh, fuck me sideways! Hearing that name coming forth sounds marvelous to the ear, no?"

He writhed in his seat in anticipation.

"Babe, there's a diner up ahead with some gas. Let's fuel up. I'm starving," Samantha said. She leaned over and kissed his cheek. "Smokey J Quarterly, huh? It does sound explicit though.

Jeff enunciate the syllables intimately, with a sinister finish that made his arms populate goosebumps.

"No, that won't work. Cause it will be niche and will die out faster than it will be born.

"Ok," Samantha said. 'Then what do *you* really want?" She cleared her throat and channeled some grandeur. "As the new editor-in-chief of this fine literary establishment, let it be known, that on this very day—"

"You sound ridiculous," Jeff said, smiling.

"Shut up, my dear king. Don't you want your decree known to all of your vassals and peasants?"

"Yes."

"Then, your highness, the name shall be…"

"Pollination. Station."

***

They never made it to California. They found a small apartment complex outside Phoenix, Arizona they called home. Once they counted their savings, they settled on a modest 800 square foot, 2-bedroom apartment for a fair price. It was discounted because the previous tenant, a 90-year-old WW2 veteran, died in the master bedroom.

"No worries! The entire unit has been sanitized!" the shifty landlord said, sweating bullets in an extremely chilled office. Their neighbors were all older; 58 was the average. Aside from their downstairs neighbor, who was a 20-year-old Mexican man that knew broken English, they were the youngest. It was red, all red. Red shingles and a clay porch covered with a sandblasted tin roof. One of the shutters was pivoting on a single screw, rocking to the motion of the late-spring breeze.

There was a mania of odd sounds emitting from Jeff's improvised office while Samantha unabashedly unpacked their possessions. Their housewares, that were donated by her family as hand-me-downs, were arranged in their apartment by movers, who were also paid by her family. A motley of furniture and appliances from the entire Cold War era began surfacing from their cardboard shelters. Despite her bountiful dowry, Samantha's displeasure grew with the intricacies of the assembly; Allen wrenches were not her forte. As the pieces clunked on the weathered hardwood, her brow dribbled on. Samantha was on the brink of losing control. She looked over at the door where Jeff resided and immediately rescinded her animosity. She came to New Mexico with good will; Jeff came with a backpack and a dream, and she respected his profound vision.

"Sam, come here. I have to show you this!" Jeff shouted. It was muffled, yet one could hear the elation in his voice.

She opened the door to find Jeff prostrate in the empty room with his laptop whirring, papers all over even taped on the walls. It was a strange sight, but for the first time in a while, she saw his smile again, the same smile she noticed that pivotal day in the lecture hall.

"What is it?"

"It's done! The press is up and running with a website."

"Oh! Let me see!"

Samantha crouched down to view the highly anticipated site. However, she was underwhelmed when all she saw was a single page with an image and two lines of text. The text read:

SOON. WE TAKE FLIGHT INTO SKIES OF LEAD AND WATER OF ANCIENTS/ POLLENATION STATION, THE NEW LITERARY POETIC.

An abstract image of an anatomical heart foregrounded a neutral, almost cloudlike, background, but didn't appear to be worth all the effort.

"How nice," she lied.

"Isn't it an eyecatcher?"

"Sure is." She looked at a small play button. "What's that for?"

"Watch!"

Jeff clicked the button and some scratchy electronic music blared on the small speakers. The image began to spin on center and took the shape of a diamond. For about two minutes this enamoring display occurred until the music faded and the image assumed its original form. Samantha's grimace spoke for itself.

"What do you think? This new press will grab the attention of everyone. When we start promoting the talent of dozens, they will be flocking to us. We will rake in the views and once we make books, you best be sure--"

"Jeff, it seems nice, but it's a bit too early in the life cycle to have high aspirations. Take a few days to fine tune it and to gather another page or two. Having a cover page is nice, but doesn't seem like it's too effective with no other place to go."

"That's what you think," he laughed. "This is only the beginning."

"I *just* said that," Samantha said, sharply.

"What's wrong with you?"

"Look. I'm just trying to get our new home put together! I mean you lock yourself in this empty room for nearly six hours while I'm trying to assemble furniture that has seen more rust than our car. All I want is to get situated first. Can't you put this off until later?"

"But this is important, Sam."

She kicked a pile of paper.

"You are ridiculous! We just graduated college and moved in together! Why can't you just help me with a *few* things around the house, goddammit!"

She crumpled to the floor and began weeping.

"It's like high-school all over again. Samantha, do this while I go to the casino. Samantha, I need you to pay this bill because I spend too much money on booze at the bar. Samantha, go to the store for groceries while I fuck this bitch to fill the void of divorcing your mother!"

Jeff blinked, feeling the strong neuroticism. He grasped her and let her finish the tirade at the crux of his arm. He wasn't akin to this side of her but a nagging paternal feeling washed over him.

"It's fine. I will help you. The press can wait."

"Promise?"

"Yes, promise. It won't take that long anyway."

Her eyes red were bloodshot but a smirk rose on her cheeks.

"Oh, you think so? You haven't seen my true powers!"

Sixteen

After a few hours of combined effort, Jeff and Samantha organized their apartment. It was modest for their tastes; Jeff was a frugal man at heart.

"All set but the toiletries!" Samantha cheered, hugging her sweaty boyfriend.

He turned his head to receive a peck on the lips.

"It looks really good, baby," Jeff said.

He marveled at the amount of furniture they had in each partitioned room. At Samantha's supervision, they seemingly doubled their occupiable spaces. In the living room, the couch was in the middle, with a 6-foot bookshelf on the left-hand side, thus creating a reading nook by a window. A fireplace flue catty-cornered the area, which served as a surround and a third "wall". If one was to sit with their back to the flue, they would have a window to their left, a bookcase to right, and a clear path to the bedroom hall. On the right-hand side, a knee-wall throttled the dining room entrance to three-foot-wide. The dinette set had a window adjacent to the head of the table. The kitchen was a few paces behind the table; a single-file walkway between appliances funneled to the entrance.

"See, it wasn't so bad. Just needed my man to do the grunt work!"

"Yes, *grunting* indeed."

The couple took a seat in the kitchen, opening water bottles.

"I interned at an interior architect's firm last year."

"Really?"

"How do you think I was able to arrange the reading nook? Wasn't by chance."

"Interesting."

"I was *obsessed* with "The Little Room" by Madeline Yale Wynne. I envisioned being one of the sisters. Always bickering about furniture...I guess that's the woman I am growing into." She giggled profusely.

"I can see that."

"Hell, I bet Poe would've been involved with home decor. While everyone was obsessing over the 'death' in "The Masque of the Red Death", I'm here ogling over those chic little bedrooms! Like c'mon, I would sleep in all of them if I had the chance."

"You have a point. He does describe buildings and interiors well. Amontillado, Usher—"

"It's a matter of efficiency. Here we are turning a measly 800 square foot apartment into what seems like 1,200. Partitions create separate 'rooms', certain paint designs can also give the appearance of elongation or width."

"All this knowledge about design, yet you devoted two semesters to write a thesis on the Shelly's?"

"You bet your lumberjack ass I did!" Samantha tugged lightly on Jeff's bird nest of a beard. His throat gurgled like a meowing cat.

"I'm starving. Let's grab some dinner."

"Okay," Samantha said. She reached for her purse on the canary yellow end table. Jeff's phone illuminated and chimed multiple times.

"Can you grab that for me?"

"*No,* mister. Dinner without phones tonight."

"Ah, you always do this to me. I have things to attend—"

Samantha pulled the battery out of his phone and dropped it gently in her purse. A metallic cling emitted.

"I have a mousetrap in there, so don't even try!"

"You're bluffing."

"Wanna try?" she contested, opening her purse wide to reveal the contraption ready to snap onto his fingers.

Jeff smirked. "You. Are such a cun—"

"*Cunning* girlfriend, I know!"

She whisked her body in a swooping motion towards the front door and flung it open. The knob banged against the wall, leaving a circular indentation. By the time Jeff laced his shoes, she was in the driver's seat. The rumble of the aged engine amalgamated with Jeff's stomach, creating a chorus.

***

It was 10:30 when Jeff and Samantha returned. He, with a bloated stomach from cheap domestic beer and quesadillas, retreated to his study while Samantha chatted with a college friend in the living room. He finally reconnected his phone and immediately went to his Glanceagram account. The notifications blazed through his feed like a strobe light: thousands of likes here, hundreds of followers there. He went to his messages and immediately began chatting with 'moonbae1050', who was his latest fascination. She was a self-proclaimed avant-garde nude expressionist and would tease him with bare breasts with enough pixelization to abide by the guidelines. She was also in the process of being a 'literary moon thing' with the vastly growing Pollination Station.

She, along with other Glanceagram sensations, were being spoon fed likes and followers for months, with the lofty aspirations of being published in *The New Joker* and beyond. Jeff was no stranger to the social media marketing ploys of purchasing fraudulent followers and cursive fonts to pump their egos with the digital equivalent of morphine. They were all his subjects and plotted out their personas like that of professional wrestling. It was unethical, yes, but Jeff's digital gatekeeping persona was able to mold their aspirations to his liking. He was, at least in his neurotic sense, the architect. He appealed to the masses of Glanceagram, thus equating an enormous capital; Jeff was raking in hundreds from the site pre-orders that had the same minimalist book designs as the posts.

Jeff could contrive the most convincing book descriptions while sporting nearly a $20 price tag. Taking a step back from his phone, he surveyed the rusty paper trimmer, rickety office printer, and reams of mismatched paper her decided to make some infrastructure upgrades. As if a bolt of lightning landed on the top of his head, he jumped on the computer and found an online printing service. Wholesale costs were incredibly low, and with the increasing flood of followers to his site, and credits for royalty-free photos at his disposal, Jeff was nearly invincible, that is until his phone vibrated and a message received by his older brother read:

Jeff. Father has died. Call me.

"What do you mean you don't want to see him?" Samantha shouted. Her voice echoed in the kitchen as Jeff sat at the table with his head in his hands. "Jeff, please. Talk to me for just a minute."

Still nothing.

"Look, babe. I'm not sure what makes you loathe him, but we only get one set of parents, as corny as that sounds."

Still, not a word from Jeff's mouth. Samantha became infuriated.

"Jeffrey! For the last time—"

"He used to beat me."

"What?" She said, taken aback.

"He...used to whip me. With a leather belt. I have nightmares still of it."

"So, like, discipline, right?"

Jeff rose, rustling the chair and rocking the table.

"No, Samantha. Like out of his own psychotic means."

"I... I don't understand."

"He was an alcoholic. My older brother and sister fled the house as soon as they turned eighteen and didn't give a flying fuck about me or my mother. Nope. They made their rite of passage and never looked back. He just took out his anger on me."

"Jeff, I'm...so sorry."

Samantha reached in for a hug but he turned his shoulder, shuddering.

"He would go after my ass the most. He would only stop when he saw specks of blood protruding from my shorts. I had such a hard time focusing at school because I couldn't sit still.

Samantha moved in closer but dared not touch Jeff in such a vulnerable state. He wept in place.

"Why did he chase my family away, Sam? Why...couldn't he just...love me?"

His trembling knees gave way. Onto the floor he went, curling up and crying uncontrollably. Samantha could only imagine the horrors that were resurfacing.

"Can I?" Samantha whispered.

Jeff continued to sob, tightening his curl.

Samantha didn't respond with words. She, too, got down onto the cold vinyl flooring and clutched Jeff from behind. His tension subsided as he felt her hands encircling his trauma. He could feel her warming breath on his neck.

"Thank you," Jeff said. His voice was faint and content."

"I love you."

"I know you do."

They remained that way for several minutes. Their breathing synchronized. Then, out of the silence, Jeff's phone began chirping; more messages were coming in. He stirred, yet Samantha would not let go.

"Now, will you go see your father?"

"Will you come with me?"

"Yes, of course. This may be what you need, Jeff. Closure."

"But, my mother still—"

"She will understand."

Seventeen

Jeff's word remained true. He purchased the flight tickets that very night. They flew into Dallas and drove down to the family home about twenty miles south. The dirt driveway and surrounding lawn were packed with cars. The home was two stories and moss grew on the northern side and some siding was in disrepair. The flagpole sported the Texas state flag underneath the stars and stripes. It was very orthodox. Jeff and Samantha appeared to be the last ones to arrive.

"Alright," Jeff said. He shifted his collar. "Now the fun begins."

He was dressed in a black suit with pinstripes and a burgundy handkerchief in the lapel. He tidied up his beard, yet kept his hair long and slick. Samantha matched him with a burgundy dress and lipstick.

As they approached the home, a group of men drinking canned beer waved them down. They were all wearing black cowboy hats, tipping them in accordance. Jeff half-bowed. His uncle, Frank, embraced him. He was a large man and his arms provided a brief sanctity.

"Jeffy. Long time, no see. Surprised you made it."

"I had to do what I had to do."

"Understood. Your mother is a mess. We have her sedated though."

"I see."

"Good day, madam," Frank said cordially.

"Frank, my girlfriend, Samantha."

She shook his hand in silence.

"Can I offer Y'all a beer?"

"That would be good," Jeff said.

The three stood on the porch. In a few minutes, Jeff nearly drank the entire can.

"It was a heart attack," Frank said. His tone was ominous.

"As I assumed."

"Had hypertension as well. The coroner still hasn't told us if he was doin' any drugs."

"Let's, uh, hope not," Jeff lied.

"Here, go in. See your momma."

Frank opened the screen door for the couple. Inside, a muted conversation arose from the rooms of the house. A single hall ran down the length, separating the kitchen and living areas. As Jeff stepped into the kitchen, the women collectively went silent. His mother sat at the counter, drinking some sort of elixir. She was flanked by his brother and sister who frowned at his appearance. Jeff's mother turned to face him, and staring with bloodshot eyes, furrowed her brow.

"The fucking baby is back home I see!"

"Hello, Maribel."

"So, are you back to beg for some of the life insurance, huh?"

"I'm here to give my old man my final respects."

"You're full of shit," Maribel said.

Jeff turned red.

"Mother, you know damn well where you stand with me and all I've been through."

"Jeffrey now's not the time," his brother, Ryan, said.

"Fuck you, Ryan."

"Hey, hey!" Kendall, his sister, interrupted. "Watch with the language."

"Nice to see you too, Ken," Jeff groaned.

"All you had to do was respect *our* wishes, Jeff. You know the hardships your father and I went through, yet you still asked and asked and asked."

"Why does this have to do with my dead father, mother?"

She rose, staggering in her flats. Maribel was overweight, yet carried decades of intangible weight on her shoulders. The elixir didn't seem to have any effect."

"Y'know, Jeffrey, if you came all this way to look at your father's urn, then do what you must and leave us the hell alone. You are not welcome back here, ever!"

Samantha, who stood diagonally to Jeff, inserted herself into the conversation.

"Ma'am, Jeff didn't do any harm. Believe me, he was torn apart when he got the news."

"And who's this little harlot? You surely don't look Christian to me!"

"Excuse me?" Samantha said.

"What a wonderful introduction! Now you go and step on my girlfriend's toes too?"

Maribel, Ryan, and Kendall produced three equal frowns. If the ceiling wasn't attached to the walls, it surely would've burst right off. Suddenly, Frank entered the fray.

"C'mon now! Are we not all Button's here? Jeffy, leave your momma be. Maribel, please relax."

The guests, who were very much inundated with strife, found ways out of the kitchen.

Jeff growled. "Show me to my father, Frank, please."

"Right this way. On the patio."

Maribel spat at Jeff's feet as he passed. They made eye contact for the final time; a menacing glare was exchanged that made them seem unrelated in the furthest degree. Samantha followed suit, holding Jeff's shoulder. On the patio, a sparse number of guests with drinks in hand parted ways. Atop a pillar of marble, a dull silver urn stood atop. Jeff guffawed as if the ornate obelisk was a taunt from the grave. Below was a verse from the Bible chiseled into the pillar:

'Brothers and sisters, we do not want you to be uninformed about those who sleep in death so that you do not grieve like the rest of mankind, who have no hope. For we believe that Jesus died and rose again, and so we believe that God will bring with Jesus those who have fallen asleep in him'

1 Thessalonians 4: 13-14

"And I'm the one wallowing in frivolity," he said to Samantha. She was motionless.

Below the scripture, on a separate chest height pillar adorned with flowers, stood a picture of his father, in good health It looked dated to Jeff. He had chestnut hair wavy and long like his own. His cheeks were tinted light pink and his brown eyes were complemented with crow's feet in the corners. He had a matching goatee which was cropped and prim. His trapezius muscles bulged at the white shirt and jacket. Samantha looked at him; she swallowed hard at Jeff's twitching face. It was at that moment that Jeff wished to grab his father by the neck and strangle him, to stare deep into the eyes that brandished so much pain. Yet, as he began to sweat, a crisp breeze blew into the yard, cooling his neck. It was an ethereal kiss, which was surreal enough to believe. He knew exactly how to feel and that was one of benevolence.

He caressed the urn, allowing the honed roundness to stimulate his fingertips. His hands made their way to the picture, grabbed it and brought it in tight to his chest. Jeff inhaled the air liked it was his dying breath, held it in for what seemed like an eternity, and exhaled, allowing a portion of his soul to be carried away to parts unknown. He set the picture back inside the flower halo and stepped back a few paces. Samantha hugged him from the side and kissed his cheek.

"Thank you, Jeffy. I'm sure he is thankful, too."

"Let's hope," Jeff said.

He turned to the patio door, noticing his family watching him. Jeff did not wish to pursue another fight.

"Frank, please watch over my mother. I'll call her later."

"Y'all will make amends?"

"Maybe so, but not for a while. I'll see us out of the yard."

"As you wish. I'll let them know you mean well."

They hugged Frank individually. Samantha headed for the gate but was halted by their elongated moment. She noticed Frank whispering something into Jeff's ear, which he acknowledged with a nod. Frank slapped his arms lightly and departed into the house.

"I need a drink, babe," Jeff sighed.

She took his arm as he strode toward the rental.

"On me."

As they left Jeff's family home, she continued to ponder in silence on what was said. She was afraid to overstep her bounds. Jeff turned on the radio and exited the driveway, kicking up a plume of dirt in the process. Samantha cranked her seat back to take a nap to the melody of Pink Floyd's, "Comfortably Numb". As she was on the brink of slumber, torn down from the hostile encounter from earlier, Jeff spoke aloud, almost as if the comment wasn't directed at anyone.

"I need a haircut."

Samantha rustled. "What's that, babe?"

"Haircut. All of it. The beard too."

"That's…surprising."

"Yes, it is," he said, still maintaining a sturdy gaze on the road ahead. His hand abnormally tight on the steering wheel. "But it has to happen. Time for a change."

"It's from earlier, isn't it?"

Jeff didn't respond.

Eighteen

With Phase 1 off his mind, Max checked his Glanceagram account and saw that he was over two million followers. This almost brought a smile to his face, but despite an increase in sales of his real poetry books, he was already growing bored. Max took a swig of a Rolling Rock.

"I guess I will wait. Doubt Julie ever says anything to me," Max said.

The rise of 'pop poetry' was sweeping the nation with 'Instapoets' leading the front. Left and right, a new star or starlet was compiling dishonest press about how 'original' they were vis a vis their peers. Max pulled up an article from the Bluffington Bias, praising newcomer, Johnny Danger, as the next 'big' poet to come from the echo chamber.

"Yeah, I just keep writing and fortune comes to me," Max read verbatim. "I just inked a major publishing deal with Smith & Anderson in NYC, all thanks to my prolific quotes…ugh, what a hack!" Max envisioned Danger's book in the big corporate bookstores, full of blank space and universal plagiarism.

"That piece of shit will be sitting next to greats such as Rimbaud and Tennyson," Max said. His stomach churned; the bathroom was needed. After relieving himself, Max went back to his room and noticed that he had a text message from Paul.

Hot damn! We sold a thousand books in the last week…hope you get this brah.

Max's grin went ear to ear, a gleam in his eye followed. He opened the window to relieve himself of the stale air he resided in for days. With only a week left before he had to move off campus, Max knew the upcoming three phases would take an eternity to complete. It still incensed him, especially the disdain his family would have over his alleged dropping out. For the first time, Max began to question what he was doing with his life, and an existential dread came over him that would have made Kierkegaard smile with pride. One week to change it all. Just one more week.

***

One of the first people Max met when he set foot on campus was Juan Martinez, a custodian at Texas Tech. Max always went out of his way to visit with Juan and ask about his family. Not only did Max like making friends with people that others might view as the dregs of society, he knew someone like Juan could help him out when needed.

"How's it going, señor Max?" Juan said, spotting his favorite student walking across campus.

"Things are good, and how is the family? Max started off with a cordial question, yet there were bigger motives at hand.

"Good. I just bought them a room back home. No more living in the shed."

"Wonderful. Hey, can I ask you for a favor?"

"Sure."

"I and a few friends want to throw one last party before we leave. I'm wondering if you might get us a key to the admin building."

"I don't know Max. They are having that big banquet there soon."

"I know, but we're just going to have a few beers and reminisce about old times. We are graduating soon, may never see each other again."

"Why the admin building?" Juan scratched the back of his head.

"It's where we all first met, besides it's only going to be a couple of hours." Max got on his knees. "Please, Juan. I'll buy you a case of Corona or whatever you like."

Juan rolled a mop handle in his hands then grabbed the key from the ring.

"I guess only for you Max, being you're one of the few that's been nice to me around here. You be careful though, they got cameras everywhere. Make sure I get the key back afterward. You know where my office is right?"

"I sure do, and thanks, Juan. This really means the world to me."

Juan smiled and watched as Texas Tech's most eccentric student walked away.

"Max is a good guy…what could go wrong?"

***

Chancellor Henry Rails sliced his drive into a pot bunker. He threw the driver in some knee-high brush.

"Who is the son of a bitch that designed this course? And even worse, I'm named after this bitch." Rails realized that the donors were playing with him, but was too occupied on his smartphone to hear him bitching about Texas Tech University's golf course.

"What did you say, Chancellor?" Brett Summers looked up from his phone. He wasn't smiling.

"I said who is the bastard that designed this cesspool of a golf course?" Rails grabbed his eight iron, attempting to get out a bogie.

"Sorry sir, don't you remember it's that Scottish fella…what's his name again?"

"Well, that Limey bastard fucked up, I know you're known around the Regents as "Deep Pocket Summers", but as you know for the first time in over a decade the university is in the red."

"I know Chancellor. How much do we need?"

"We'll talk about that later, now climb down that ladder and fetch my ball out of that bunker."

"Yes, sir."

Summers waddled in the direction of the sand trap. Rail's phone rang. He squinted as he tried to answer it.

"What the fuck is this? An email from a student? I see…interesting…a case of academic fraud...and with that poet? Oh, wait until I talk to Waters about this. I should have fired his ass long ago."

***

Linda Rails sat in the living room of her husband's estate. It wasn't easy being the Chancellor's wife, but she had an image to maintain. The idea of marriage died many years ago and Linda knew of her husband's infidelity. She never took legal action but wasn't pleased with the welfare of her daughter, Kasey. The flip side of the coin, being he wasn't the only one that fooled around. There was the pool boy Julio last year but over the years she couldn't remember all her lovers. There wasn't much to do with her time, besides, take her exercise and spend her hotheaded husband's money. The only solace in Linda's life was her precious teenage daughter Kasey, who she gave birth to in her late 30's.

Linda never told Henry that Kasey wasn't his child. In fact, she even kept the secret from her daughter. On the day of her birth, Henry thought Kasey didn't look like anyone else in the family, which she cautiously worded around, stating that she resembled her own mother, which remained the pillow talk opinion ever since.

"Oh, my dear, Kasey, can you fetch me my crochet?" Linda yelled up the stairs.

"Ugh, fine," Kasey moaned from her bedroom. "Wish you'd find a new hobby."

She lay on her bed reading one of her favorite poetry books, *Sugar and Spice,* by the dreamy, Ethan Lane, another Instapoet. His book had become the rage at school, emitting a 'prince charming' appeal with empty aphorisms and promises of elementary feminism. Kasey was enjoying being a high school sophomore and her mother dumped money into her allowance at a whim. Kasey and her friends spent most of their time at Barney & Jules, drinking sugar-filled coffee drinks and buying dozens of books. They would buzz about, dreaming in a mystifying group at the author pictures of the male poets, while simultaneously scoffing the female. They were secretly jealous of their fame, claiming that they were trying to get in their pants.

Although Ethan Lane was her favorite, the most popular Instapoet was the mysterious Tyler Young. He had the most followers, and it seemed every girl at her school was talking about him. Kasey felt like cheating on Ethan so she could crack the code Tyler presented. Plus, he had a dreamy beard that went down to his pecs. She desired to make him hers one day, and she had all the money to get him.

"Hi, like do you have Tyler Young's book?" Kasey asked an employee.

"Nope. It's been back-ordered for two weeks. I'm sorry, miss."

"Oh, sucks." She pulled out two $100 bills from her purse. "Would you have, like, any more in the back?"

The employee perked up. "Let me just go see."

As she was waiting, she perused Glanceagam that Tyler was selling his book. Even though the book's author was Max Wilson, she ordered it right away.

"Dirty Panties and Pela...pegasus? Sounds so hot," Kasey said to her friends. They got jealous and instantly ordered them too. The employee emerged from the back with a small stack of books.

"Miss, we have 4 copies that were reserved—"

The girls had left with their drinks half drunk and still on the table.

Nineteen

Samantha could hardly recognize Jeff when he came home. His beard was gone. His scraggly hair was cut and rolled into a man-bun. He wreaked of high-end cologne and was wearing a royal blue sportcoat, brown tapered shoes, and a white collared shirt, which was undone one button too much; his chest hair poked through. His eyes hid behind mirrored aviator sunglasses, which Samantha saw her own mouth agape in.

"And who are you supposed to be, Mr. Hollywood?"

Jeff chuckled, removing his glasses. "I'm a publisher."

"Of what, exactly?"

"Well," Jeff took a seat, spreading his legs in stifling thin pants. "Remember how I told you about Glanceagram?"

"Uh, I think so."

"I found a way to get my publishing company over 10,000 followers in only a few days. I've been getting at least fifty messages a day about how to get published. I can't answer them all. I need only the highest followings."

"And who is that?"

"I had coffee with a guy Ethan Lane. He's a hit from California. See, look we took a selfie."

Samantha looked at his phone. A frown formed on her face.

"You both...look *exactly* the same."

"I know, right? We're bros now, what can I say? He came all the way to chat with *me.* He already self-published a book and wants to join forces with my following to publish another."

"What's his work like?"

"It's genius, actually. He writes epigrams. Short and sweet. He says he already locked down a demographic; a cult following, really!"

"And that is?"

"YA, y'know, young adult?"

"High Schoolers, Jeff." Samantha groaned. "I'm scrolling through his Glanceagram now. Are you sure you want to publish this? It looks like greeting cards courtesy of a hipster typewriter."

"No, see this is how I plan it. We get him to jumpstart our following even more. He sells thousands of books, maybe do some customized poetry pieces for the holidays and such. Then we gather even *more* poets and before you know it, we are in Barney & Jules. Nationwide!"

"So, where do the 'awards' come in? I'm not sure how this industry works, but I'd hate to see you pursue a cash grab. You're smart and radical at times. That moment you stood up against that sleaze in class...well, just don't lose sight of that drive to be a maverick, not a plastic fluke."

Jeff regarded her statement with a peck on the forehead. He was confident that things were going to crest from mediocre to outstanding in a matter of months. All he knew was to publish, to make poetic expression his top priority. Possibly, he was on the cusp of a big break.

***

The ensuing days proved to be bountiful for Jeff's Pollination Station. He was preparing for the pilot publication, *Tears on the Cheese Plate.* The author was restrained from promoting, for he wanted to have a grand release on Christmas. He knew the holidays would bolster the sales, offering package deals for any interested author at half off. He gazed at his sparse website, matching the color scheme with autumn, and played his favorite tune from Tame Impala through a media player.

There were only two menus: one led to the preorder of the book, the other to a support website for inquiries and press. Jeff had no idea the minimalism would draw in so much attention. The website's revenue totaling in the thousands; thousands of real dollars people were dumping into the business account. Jeff drooled. His mind blurred the rationale for he was incensed and vigorous. His plot was beginning to complete the circle of completion.

"This will show them. Those hacks at Texas Tech don't know what's about to hit them. This book will be a poetic masterpiece."

All the while, Samantha remained outside the room, her ear pressed against the door. She heard mumbles, maniacal typing of the keyboard, and of course, Jeff's intent. She sighed, tugging at her sweater. It was as if she was being choked by the wool.

"My man!" Jeff shouted with glee. Samantha could hear only bits and pieces.

"Your book is coming along nicely. Just a bit more sketches to implement...yes, preorders are going…what? You bet! I will have to fly out there and have a launch party…Venice Beach? Fuck yeah! Did you get the dope under control? And hookers? Sweet, can hardly wait!

He hung up and resumed clicking. He was oblivious to reality or the suspicion of plagiarism, and as the 316-page book became formulated with center-justified aphorisms and sexually explicit doodles, he could hardly hear the muffled whimpers of Samantha right outside.

***

Ethan Lane sat in his loft apartment that overlooked Venice Beach. It wasn't his apartment but belonged to his latest fling, Ashley. Ethan never paid for anything but was able to live off fangirl after fangirl for days if not weeks on end. The young millennial women—and some divorced housewives in their 40's—followed Ethan's minimalistic poetry on Glanceagram and would lay the red carpet out for him. Rarely would he entertain the option of sex, yet scores advanced on him, yet his melancholic nature kept them at bay with mere servitude. They dared not interfere with his 'artistic expression'. It was almost as if Ethan developed his own religion, for all the fans he stayed at knew everything he did or said.

Ethan was seeing some growth on his page, but he was jealous of Tyler Young. He was engaged in a silent competition with him, vying to get a celebrity re-post as soon as possible. Ethan tried not to dwell on it, besides, Jeff mentioned that his publisher would buy him followers once things got rolling. The ink was barely dry on the publishing contract and Ethan already had delusions of being the greatest poet in the world. Glanceagram was changing poetry and Ethan wanted to be king. Ethan knew his work wasn't good enough to get published anywhere, especially since he was community college dropout. He was chastised by his English professors, which drove him to the administration. Ethan knew his poetry sucked, but none of that mattered now; his vendetta was too huge to disregard.

"Dear, would you like more chamomile tea?" a topless woman with dreadlocks said, walking by his bedroom door.

"No, thank you. The muses do not call for that now…but a whiskey on the rocks does."

Twenty

Back at the Barry Motel, Ray Lester was oblivious to the electronics that Max stripped away. He was aloof to most practices—primarily focusing on the cash and 'attractions'—and even forgot the whole operation that Max implemented. Once the keyboard and cameras were gone, Lester brought the old cash register back and loaded it with paper for the next transaction. He didn't, however, forget the banquet.

It's almost time," Ray Lester said, pushing a broom.

"What you say?" Suzie asked.

"I say, it almost time. You ain't got in your hearing aid, do you? Listen, its almost time for the big party remembers Max invite us?"

"Who's Mag?" Suzie mumbled through her toothless mouth.

"The scholar! Now, go git Patricia and Leroy and here some money to go shopping. I want us looking good for this banquet so get something nice. I already got my wedding suit; ain't been worn in thirty years but it sharp. Got them fancy ruffles and what not."

"Shop? I ain't been shopping in years. I do need a new dress, been wearing this raggedy ass one for years." Suzie tugged on the front of her dress nearly exposing her saggy breasts.

"Lord a 'mercy, go find Patricia and Leroy and get yo' ass down to the thrift shop and remember ta get something nice!"

Suzie crept into the next room.

"I wonder why I not hear from Max, he probably so busy with them books," Lester said, fumbling with the keyboard. "Make no matter, already got tickets to the party on Friday, and we see Max there. Wonder what kind of grub they gonna have? I sure is hungry."

The door swung open and none other than the fat man walked in.

"I want room one seventeen. What's the special?" Dean Waters asked.

"Yes sir, we got a deal, real nice China doll," Lester said.

"That sounds perfect," Waters said, clicking his tongue on the inside of his cheek.

"Yes sir, I send her down to your favorite room right away."

***

Max twirled around in his desk chair and felt good knowing he only had two days left at Texas Tech. Lester called to let him know he possessed the tape.

"This is too bizarre. I almost don't want to see it," Max said.

He reluctantly rolled the footage on his laptop, nearly vomiting at the sight. 'Quality control' he rationalized, but Waters was way too perverse and couldn't watch another second.

"Ok, that'll do," he said, copying the grotesque film onto a USB drive. Max walked to his closet to dust off the 'ninja costume'. Max wore it on Halloween when he went to a sorority party with Julie and now he needed to disguise himself, when he snuck into the administration building, the night before the banquet. Julie popped into his head again, and when he put her in place of the prostitute, he shuddered. No way would she submit to Water's deviance, would she?

The plan was to sneak in and add a few 'party favors' to enhance the evening for the distinguished guests. It seemed everything was falling into place, and if successful, it would go down as the most infamous prank in Texas Tech's history. Max looked at himself in the mirror. He had put on weight since the Halloween party that he regretfully attended and the costume seemed two sizes too small. His gut hung out perfectly rounded and even the mask felt like a vice on his enormous head.

"This is what Custard must have felt like before the natives relieved him of his misery," Max said, turning to his profile.

"It'll have to do…maybe a few less Rolling Rocks."

Max gasped trying to pull up the spandex pants that exposed some of his butt crack.

"I will have a nice letter to send to the manufacturer after this is over," Max groaned.

He trotted to the kitchen, his suit making a *swishing* sound as he walked.

"At least the party favors are a go," Max said as he opened the mini-fridge with the expired dozen eggs and the tub of rancid catfish bait. The plan would be to put both in the air conditioning vent and crank it up. The place would be stinking to high heaven by the time the guests arrived.

The security guard at the admin building was either eating doughnuts or out on patrol, so getting inside would be easy. Max surveyed the area and saw that the coast was clear, his beady eyes protruding through two holes cut in a black bandana. He crouched behind a bush and let one of the campus security vans pass. He was certain that in his earlier years, he ended up in at least one of each van. He darted to the front door, performing a lackluster somersault to the stoop. Max wheezed, checking on the bait; he would've surely smelled the eggs by now if some cracked in his performance.

Max staggered to the door and unlocked it with Juan's key. There wasn't an alarm or even the sight of anyone in the immediate vicinity. He had no idea what to do about the cameras rolling.

"Shit. I should've asked Juan about the server room," he whispered.

He crept to the security window, poking his head around the closed blinds. Empty. He squeezed his way into the cramped office, lined with shelving units and a single stool for a smaller person to sit, and found the switch for the cameras.

"Bingo," Max said, flipping it, and seeing the few monitors go blank with a 'SIGNAL LOST' notification. He was so close. He shuffled like a shadow down the hallway, until he got to the janitor's closet, which was conveniently unlocked. Max flipped the light switch and saw what he was looking for: a fold-down aluminum latter that led to the banquet hall on the upper level. Max chuckled.

"Juan, you marvelous bastard."

He ascended the ladder and flipped open the grate of the air conditioning duct. He attempted to climb in like a demented trapeze artist, balancing his girth on one foot on the ladder rung. His ankle made popping noises as he maneuvered the eggs and bait into the vent. He cracked some eggs for good measure and descended the ladder like Zeus coming down from Mt. Olympus. He mopped down the tile floor with dirty water to prove Juan he did some work. He had one last plan. He took the stairs to the empty banquet hall. In a secluded back corner, away from the entrance and tables, he placed a video camera in a fern and played with the settings.

"No way I'm leaving here without a copy for Blutube," he said. The camera blipped and was primed and ready for the hilarity. Max locked up and went back to his dorm. He never returned the key. 'Operation Rotten Egg' was complete, with the worst of them all, 'Role the Footage', soon to take place.

***

Julie brushed her hair and stared at her reflection in the mirror above the dresser. Lately, she needed to see her reflection to know she existed. Tears trickled down her cheeks ruining her mascara. She dabbed on some more, giving her face a chalky appearance. Dean Waters had set up a meeting with her and Chang after the banquet, where he mentioned 'something urgent' needed to be discussed. Had someone discovered her lie? Perhaps, Chang ratted her out? The dire possibilities raced through her head but there was little time to dwell on her misfortune. She didn't even know what to say to the graduate students at the banquet; Waters suggested writing a speech to impress the professors coming in from the Ivy League. Apparently, if things went well, Waters mentioned he might have a job at Yale or Harvard. The pressure was on her and Chang to impress the distinguished guests and faculty, as the beacons of literary genius at Texas Tech. Julie hoped to assume the wallflower aspect so that nobody would notice, but that would be difficult since Waters told her to 'show off'. She worried he'd be monitoring her movements, almost as if her appearance was a choreography of brownnosing.

"What does he know? Just an old wrinkly pig," Julie said, looking at her juvenile speech on her laptop. It was a complete disaster. The first line read: '*Hey, Y'all. Welcome to Texas Tech...get your guns up!*' None of the out-of-town guests would comprehend the school's tagline, given the current political state of the liberal East. It reminded her of the football game a couple of years ago, where Texas Tech's mascot, 'Saddle Tramp', got loose on the field and stampeded into a stadium wall, killing itself instantly. Max always said the poor beast had snuffed itself on purpose to avoid witnessing another 2-8 season.

***

Ray Lester looked at himself in the mirror.

"Oowee, I'm looking sharp. Look at them blue ruffles…like my wedding night back in '75. Too bad it didn't work…"

"What you say?" Suzie mumbled, staring at Lester with a perplexed look on her face.

"I say shut yo' mouth! You know we 'bout to go to the party over at der school and Max be 'specting us. You ain't got yo' teeth in," Lester yelled.

"Who Mag?" Suzie mumbled.

"You wearing that raggedy ass dress again? Ain't you got something nice to wear?" Lester said as he paced in front of the mirror, checking to see that his yellow carnation was pinned in the correct place. "Find Leroy and Patricia. It time to go, and I got our tickets right here in my pocket."

"Yessir."

Leroy stumbled into the lobby with a forty ounce and plopped down in a chair with Patricia in tow, both wearing their 'Sunday clothes'. Patricia in her periwinkle dress, showing chiseled leg muscles, wrapped her arm around Leroy's faded navy jacket. His undershirt was wrinkled and spotted with bleach stains.

"We ready and I sure is hungry. Ain't that right Patricia?"

"We sure is and ain't I going to be the queen of the ball?"

"Mighty good, you both look sharp. Suzie went looking for you both, she probably lost by now. Y'all sit right here and I'll find her old ass. Then we be ready."

"I wonder if they got shrimps?" Leroy slurred.

"I hope they got catfish. I got a craving something bad," Patricia said.

**

Chancellor Rails was doing his best to impress the distinguished professors from the Ivy League; Penn to be specific. They were an entourage of esteemed academics and board members, all wearing slim-fit suits and cocktail dresses for the women. They looked foreign in the dusty town of Lubbock.

"Welcome to my university," Chancellor Rails said opening the door to the admin building. The group glimpsed at the wooden wainscot and mold-ridden vinyl tiles. Juan was busy scrubbing graffiti on a wall and welcomed them in with a lazy wave. A collective silence took over them. Rails escorted a woman up the stairs by the hand, kissing it. She withdrew it quickly.

"My apologies, Madame. Just how we do things 'round these parts."

"Sure," Doctor Weaver said. She whispered something to her associate, Professor Teuton.

They took the rickety elevator up to the banquet hall, where they were welcomed with a pungent odor.

"My goodness!" Professor Teuton said, covering his face. The servers, all donning tuxedos and dust masks, scurried around the floor, attempting to cover the hors-d'oeuvres from contamination.

"What in tarnation is going on here?" Rails shouted.

"Chancellor Rails!" a server called out. "We have a situation. Hopefully, we can rectify it before the banquet. Some animal must've gotten in overnight."

"Go figure…hurry this up! The banquet is in an hour."

Rails sent a few bussers to the mechanical room to check the vents.

"I am terribly sorry about this, Dr. Weaver, Professor Teuton, et al. I can assure you this isn't a normal occurrence, it's possible a varmint got up in the air conditioning vent. All should be fine." Sweat was popping up on Rails' forehead.

"Let us go back to the lobby until this clears up," someone from the group said. Nods and grunts of affirmation rung out and they descended back down. Rails called Waters.

"I'm bringing the VIP's back downstairs for now. You better hope they fix this," Rails muttered. He ground his teeth to dust in frustration.

In a back room near the banquet hall, Waters picked up his phone. He was leaning against the wall with his legs crossed, facing Julie and Chang. They sat in plastic chairs, reading their print-outs, dressed for a funeral. Chang's hair was combed to a coif while Julie's was curled into many locks.

"The show must go on, chancellor. I have Julie and River here. We will be good to go." Waters looked at his star pupils. "Right?"

They nodded.

"Julie, you will speak first and just be your typical perky self. River, you go on after, kiss some ass, and read some of your haikus."

"I'm…looking forward to it," Chang said. His brow was wrinkled.

"I think I'm ill," Julie said. She went to stand up, yet wobbled back onto her butt.

"Nonsense. The smell will go away and I smoothed everything over with Chancellor Rails, so don't worry about our meeting after this." Waters lied.

Chang's underarms were beginning to darken. The AC was shut off to rectify the issue, thus the creeping arid heat snuck through the many cracks of the old building.

"It's too late now, let's make the best of it. Here, take some water," Waters said, handing them over. He looked at his watch; Julie and Chang gasped with refreshment.

"We're due out in 20. Let's go over the script…"

Twenty-one

Later that day, as Samantha was away for work, Jeff was at his desk, taking the daily tallies of the site visits and, of course, the revenue. His phone was on the fritz, receiving a huge uptick in messages. He was already moving past Ethan and recruiting some other aloof poets to join his platform. He only accepted Glanceagramers with over 40,000 followers; the follow-buying formula worked more effectively at that threshold. He had a wad of 100's wrapped in a rubber band off to the corner. He smirked, knowing quite well the holidays would surge his intake.

"Wait, just wait until they see this."

He toiled into the evening, lighting a few candles next to gleaming amethyst crystals and poignant incense. A woman with the codename, 'Baefore and After', was sexting him with photos of Ethan Lane's book strategically placed around her breasts and crotch. She was the model for all the books on the page, yet she hailed from Topeka, Kansas. She fell in love with Jeff's allure and lofty dreams of being an actress in California, yet she was now dead set on becoming a book modeler. Jeff threw her a couple grand to take pictures of dummy books in all types of erotic positions. 'Exposure for you, playtime for me' he would affirm. All the while, she knew naught of his relationship. Tonight, they exchanged full frontals, uncensored. He was lost in the lust between them.

Hey partner ;)

Yes moonchild

So when will I get to go on a rodeo through Grand Canyon???

Soon. I need to push another 3 books out before Thanksgiving then we can make the canyon shake.

"Good ;) I'm like a little broke lol Gucci purse threw me over can you send me another grand please?

Of course

Oh thank you thank you! <3 You won't regret it daddyyy

Jeff took a break and reclined on the couch with a whiskey neat. He churned the liquor in his tumbler, feeling the need to please himself when lights shone through his blinds. Samantha was home. He staggered to his office to put away all the press documents, the cash, and his cock. He retreated to the bedroom and snatched a Hesse novel from a bookcase, appearing as innocuous as can be. He heard the door unlock. He heard her purse and keys *thump* on the floor. He heard her shoes, too. then silence. Jeff exhaled and began rummaging for his release. Samantha wasn't coming to bed after all. She was too busy sobbing into the couch.

***

The next day, the air conditioner in the apartment broke again. The landlord was away for a week, apparently so was Jeff. Samantha hardly saw him, and the chances she did, he was hopping in that same matte black Porsche; the same unknown driver, the same 'business expenses'. She had no idea what was going on with the press anymore and her snooping didn't overturn anything. It almost appeared that Jeff didn't have a press at all.

"He's doing a great job. He does the printing from a third party, that's why there aren't any books. Sales must be great."

She kept rationalizing to herself positive things, yet it didn't seem to make it any better, and she was always worried about Jeff. She started writing home, asking her parents if they still had her old bedding ready, asking if they would pay for a U-Haul to whisk her away from the dump she's been living in. She was catching on, though.

She was able to leave work in the afternoon on a Wednesday in hopes of intercepting Jeff. She parked her car in the neighbor's garage, as a favor, and waited at home with all the lights off, save for a single candle in the kitchen. The sunset was descending and the apartment was lathered with gray. The heard the front door jostle and in came Jeff muttering to himself. He was shocked when he laid eyes on her face.

"What are you doing here?" He said. His pupils dilated.

"I'm hot, Jeff. Very hot."

"Yes, where is the landlord?"

"Away, for a week, Jeff. I was hoping maybe you could try to fix it, given that you know the *solution* to everything."

"I'll call the repair guy tomorrow."

"Will you?" Samantha rose from her seat. "Y'know that costs money, right?"

Jeff began pacing around, deep in thought.

"You going to answer me?"

"Look, Sam, I have like 10 book projects working in my head. Trying to balance—"

"*Ten?*"

"Being worked on."

"Where? I don't see ten books." Samantha expanded her arms to show that there were no books in the kitchen.

"I have them with a confidant. Legal reasons."

"Why?"

"Can't tell you that."

Jeff made it to the office and flicked on the lights. A verbose account of obscenities followed. He dashed out, face alighted like a furnace.

"What. The fuck. Is this?" he shouted, holding up a document with a seal.

"Hope you're not mad I opened up your mail. But it looked *really* urgent, and since you're never home, I took it upon myself."

"I'm being sued? For what?"

"Tell that to your pretty Porsche driver, whoever it may be."

"This is absurd. Ok, I had to push the deadlines back a couple weeks, but people need to understand...that producing such art takes time. Our poetic endeavors are not something that can be spewed out."

"Jeff."

"It's unavoidable that sometimes we may skim over a shipment since we have thousands of orders a month, but all they need to do is query our support site. These simpletons can't decipher A from B."

"Jeff."

"This press is putting on a monumental performance here, to change poetics as we know it for the next century of—"

"Jeffrey Button!"

His monologue ceased. He slumped into a chair and groaned. His fingers were shoved into his eyes.

"I've been studying you and this press for some time now. How you didn't foresee this, is beyond me. You can't keep promising all these books to these people and expect them to not complain when they don't receive their product."

Jeff didn't respond. His phone buzzed but he didn't touch it.

"How many dollars, Jeff."

"$50,000, give or take."

"Fuck," Samantha said. She stared at the ceiling, her hands behind her head.

"And where is all this money?"

"I have maybe ten grand still. Rest is gone."

"I *knew* it! You and what's-his-face have been spending all this money. You act like I don't notice these receipts and late nights."

"It wasn't so bad at first. These artists are true geniuses and will wait months on end for a good book."

"So, where are the editorials, huh? I want to see one book, just *one*. Just so I can see how fucked you are."

Jeff fished into his drawstring bag and revealed a proof of a book. Samantha noticed the eccentric cover with a vague image that contained many triangles and possibly a tribal heart.

"Ethan Lane. He's your poster-child huh?"

Jeff nodded. His phone buzzed again.

With further inspection, Samantha noticed typos almost immediately. The short stanzas were offset too far into the spine, the font was skewed as if the printer head was wearing out, and occasionally a page number was missing.

"Jeff. Are you for real with this? It looks like shit. I'm no *publisher* like you, but these are not books I would purchase at any bookstore. What the fuck have you been doing this whole time?"

"Excuse me, but our editors slave over these things, like Latin scholars translating the Bible."

Samantha wasn't having it. She noticed his phone was now ringing.

"Who's that? It's been going off all this time."

"I don't know," he blurted, refusing to acknowledge it.

Samantha saw the name and grew furious.

"Well, if *you're* not gonna answer, I sure as fuck will!"

He wrangled her arms, furious in the pursuit to answer.

"No, no you won't!" Jeff grunted.

Within their tussle, Samantha was able to hit the answer button before it fell onto the floor. Within seconds, a high pitched, feminine voice emitted through the other end. She didn't skip a beat as if she was on an answering machine.

"Jeff, babe. Look, I don't know if I want to do this anymore. I was contacted by Clayboy and... yeah y'know that's more important than book modeling. But hey, I'll be free soon if you want to...well, y'know, in the Grand Canyon. Hope you're not mad, daddy! Ok, bye!"

Samantha, who was straddling him, reached for his throat.

"And you're *cheating on me?*" she screamed.

"No. It's not like that." He muttered, coughing at her voracious grip.

The couple struggled for a bit. Jeff managed to undo her clench but couldn't guard against a knee to the groin. He wailed on the floor.

"I... I don't know what to say." Samantha gasped. "First you hide this scheme, now you flirt with other women while I work my ass off to keep the bills paid Well, Jeff, now the tables have turned. Good luck figuring shit out, because we're done."

Samantha left the room, grabbing a trash bag filled with clothes and possessions; she was prepared. Jeff crawled into the hall.

"Samantha, you can't go. We have so much to do, so much promise."

"*Had*, Jeff. This relationship died once you estranged from your 'art'. I can't believe you lied to me after I had to defend *you* in front of your entire family. I can see where you got these genes from."

Jeff was struck by lightning. The realization of his grand facade crumbling was not just a check of reality, but a breaking of the digital wall.

"Sam, wait."

Despite rising to a knee, to repent for his action, to kneel before the goddess that knew all along, the door was slammed shut and tires squealed into the distance.

Twenty-two

Ray Lester led Suzie, Leroy, and Patricia into the banquet hall. Most of the guests were socializing in the halls and lobby; panicked bussers swirled around them like gnats to fulfill drink orders. They stared in contempt at the group, which gave the appearance of a traveling circus troupe.

"Oowee, they got shrimp and there ain't nobody in here," he said while twiddling his fingers.

"I wonder if Max throws this party for us…sure be nice of him to think of us like family," Leroy said. He was already drunk. He swiped a cosmopolitan from a tray.

"And it smell good in here…remind me of mama's cooking. Can't understand why nobody here take our tickets either. They must know we was coming. Let's get some grub. Oowee, mighty good."

"Where Mag?" Suzie said. Her walker scraped the flooring, emitting a high-pitched squeal.

"Girl, how much you had to drink?" Patricia said. She stuffed several jumbo shrimps in her mouth.

"I ain't had but a few." Suzie stumbled on the tablecloth, banging into the table. Empty wine glasses clinked, few crashed onto the floor. Lester tried to save the fruit plate, but pushed hard on the edge, sending pieces into the air.

"Dang nabbit!" Suzie said. "Damn clothes ain't what they used to be."

"Woman, go take a' seat. Max will be here soon," Lester said, shooing her to the nearest table.

"Oh, goodness. A dancefloor. Leroy, reckon we do a jig?" Patricia said, pointing at the parquet floor in the center."

Leroy belched. "Not now. Needs to settle my stomach."

Downstairs, the east-coast group was already on their third drink, finally relieved that the smell was dissipating. Chancellor Rails' armpits were stained three shades darker. He tried calling Waters but his phone was off. He was afraid that his guests would depart, so kept them distracted with outdated sporting awards. They were indifferent, viewing their Twitter feeds and other likely escapisms from the pitiful small talk.

"Do you know those four stranglers, chancellor? They don't seem…adequate for such an award. Did Waters allow them here?" Dr. Weaver said, pointing upward. Lester's voice echoed in unsatisfied ears.

"They are esteemed guests," Rails lied. He was seething within, seeing the archaic Ray Lester in *his* building after his failed negotiations. "The older couple, uh, Mr. and Mrs. Lester, donate fairly often to the university and—"

"I'm ready to catch the next red-eye out of this godforsaken place. No way in hell will Waters obtain his tenure in the Ivy League now," Professor Teuton said. He was teetering in place with a whiskey sour in one hand.

'What about Chang? Don't you want to hear him read?" Dr. Weaver asked.

"If I could be candid," Professor Teuton said. "Chang is probably *the* most overrated poet in America. His juvenile haikus have all been played out. I'd be damned if he gets another book out in the next two, no *five* years." Professor Teuton said. "And for God's sake, does this barnyard got a fan? It still reeks!"

"I suppose you're right to 'get outta dodge' and some fresh air," Dr. Weaver said while following Teuton and the others out the side door of the administration building.

"No, you cannot leave! The banquet has nearly begun!" Rails said, staggering outside. He was able to grab Dr. Weaver's shoulder. She shrugged him off and pivoted around.

"Look, Chancellor. You got 10 minutes to get your banquet under control or we will have some foul words to say to your board of directors. Got it?"

Rails' face flushed. "Yes…yes, I will. Take 15 if you want! It'll be all ready for you!"

***

Waters busted into the nearly empty banquet hall, except for Lester's gang and a few starry-eyed undergrads with delusional MFA ambitions and napkins up to their faces.

"Where the hell is everyone?" His nostrils flared. "And what is that smell?" Waters turned around to see if Chang and Julie were behind him, and saw both stumbling around holding their noses.

"I hope this goes away," Chang said.

"Yeah, you're telling me!" Julie said. She coughed a few times.

"Where are Weaver and Teuton? Rails?" Waters tuned on his phone and saw multiple voicemails and texts from Rails. His stomach dropped.

"Julie, we must go on! You're up first and the distinguished guests are due to arrive any minute. C'mon, go!" He nudged her toward the podium.

"But…I feel sick." Julie muttered.

"Here, you want a drink? Let me grab you one. Oh, waiter!" Waters shouted for a server. Julie approached the podium and unfolded her speech. Despite the abhorrent conditions, she knew once the VIP's were present, her shoe-in to academic success would be complete. She shivered but was far enough away to be unnoticeable. She tapped the mic; it whined in response.

"Hello? Is this thing on?"

A few students nodded.

"Great…well…hello and welcome to Texas Tech's Coronation Banquet!" A few claps emitted and more people in suits began filtering into the hall. Julie, for once in many months, smiled. As we say down south, 'Get yer guns up!'" She waved her hand in the air in an 'L' shape. A few chuckled.

"Guns up!" Lester yelled from the buffet table. He tossed a shrimp in the air, attempting to catch it in his mouth, but missed.

"Dammit!"

He looked around and everyone was staring at him.

"I so sorry, ma'am. I'd pick it up."

Julie laughed, her smile now ear to ear, then reset. "Tonight, we have a very special presentation for you…"

***

Chancellor Rails heard the amplified voice and summoned the east coast-group back inside.

"Y'all! We have begun. Please, hurry on up. I'll be right there."

His phone alerted him a large file being downloaded via email.

"What the fuck is this now?" Rails scrolled and saw Max Wilson as the sender. The title said, 'Thought you might like this' and noticed that there were dozens of professors—some deans of other colleges—that were CC'd in the email.

"Doesn't ring a bell."

He pulled up the attached video. After a few seconds of black, he screeched at the sight. It was Dean Waters in bed with a woman!

"Jesus H..." Rails said, dry heaving. "In all my damn years, I've never…" He took a seat on a bench with his elbows digging into his knees, clenching his sweaty forehead. There was a moment of clarity, though, when he realized that this deus ex machina fit perfectly in his plan. He stood up, with a smirk, and set his sights on the banquet.

"Oh well. It couldn't have happened to a nicer guy."

Twenty-three

Jeff didn't sleep at all that night. He attempted to make amends with his editors, but his pleas were not answered, only the He browsed his Glanceagram account. Ethan Lane had gone rogue, alerting all his fans to not purchase from his site. They listened. Word spread. The revenue ceased. Refund alerts were popping up like mosquito bites. His cash heap was low and the real fear of losing everything became a stark reality. Samantha did not respond to his elongated laments. Her phone was off and her social media deactivated.

Jeff paced around the house until the carpet was matted. Occasionally, he slithered to the window and peered through a single slat, awaiting his black Porsche to whisk him away to Mexico, or even worse, the police with a bench warrant. The sun poked through the blinds this time and he succumbed to a bout of anxiety-induced sleep.

***

He awoke around 10 AM. The front of his shirt was damp with sweat. He rose and stammered to the bathroom to puke. His kidneys ached, his face, pallid. The gig was up. He was all alone to face the repercussions before him. He did what only he imagined he could do. He peeled an apple, plopped in front of his desk, and began emailing anyone and everyone with a grievance. There were hundreds of inquiries in varying degrees of severity. He took the legal and death threats on hand first, issuing immediate payments, some orders upwards of over $50. He worked through lunchtime and into the afternoon. His phone rang a few times and screened it: 'Pinch'. Lars Berlin, that he met by happenstance at a nightclub in Phoenix, had experience in libel and small claims cases, but the scale of Jeff's vanity press had warranted even more effort from him. He was a slick guy in his late 20's. Trust fund. Northwestern University alum with honors. He fought like a maimed dog for his budding clients. Jeff nicknamed him Pinch for that reason. He pulled up the text messages.

Jeff my man hookah bar 530 sharp bring a pen and reading glasses we gonna be a while lol

***

"Samantha left me, man," Jeff moaned, exhaling a plume of blueberry-scented smoke.

"I don't think you should be concerned with her right now…" Lars said, taking the hookah hose.

There were forms on the table, along with a double order of tortilla chips and guacamole. The bustling hipster crowd mewed around them. The clacking of keyboards and even typewriters superseded the pouring of coffee and hissing of the panini press. Jeff, who was back to his stringy facial hair, was feeling uncomfortable being immersed in the lounge. Despite being the same age group of his immediate peers, he felt haggard and archaic. His mental state was that of a mid-40-year-old facing bankruptcy. He felt the fraudulence around him like a bubble and was meek in pushing his finger into it, protruding into the confines of a socio-economic reality. He realized that these people were his audience, his clients. He even saw a woman wearing a tee shirt with an Ethan Lane quote. Jeff's forehead wrinkled, his lips pushed forward. He even felt tears beginning to well in the corners of his eyes.

"...get your money right, take care of this press, and move on. If she's still around that is." Lars nudged Jeff out of his daydream. "Yo, are you even listening to me?"

"Yes, I... I will handle my business first." He shuffled on the plush sofa. "Ok, where do we get started?"

***

The duo worked fastidiously into the night as many of the regular patrons disbanded. Jeff continued to read papers and signing the bottom, over and over. A group of boisterous women entered. They were having a bachelorette party and Lars was getting distracted, tossing some legal documents to the side.

"Ah, don't worry about this one."

"Just sign here, yeah. That'll do."

Jeff sneered. Page 150 of 264. He wasn't fond of Lar's anymore.

"How much longer, Lars?"

"Almost...like 10 mins. Here you want a hit?"

"Nah, I just want to get out of here already," Jeff said.

"Jeffy, buddy! Why the long face?"

"I'm alone. Before you know it, the landlord will be asking questions. I'll end up falling behind since I don't have an income. I'll be evicted. My family doesn't give a fuck about me anymore." Jeff stared into the smoldering coals. "She was my rock while I got it all situated. Now I have neither."

Lars cupped his shoulder, nudging him. "Bro, you can stay with me! I'm about to settle for a nice condo in Venice Beach. I got you. Your own bedroom *and* bathroom. All you need to do is sign this last page. C'mon man, you need this. You need *me*."

Jeff fumbled the pen in his hand and stared at the contractual document. He imagined he could come out of this alive, with maybe some cash left over to build security for himself. He imagined living a humble, yet sound life in California, leaving behind the sins of his past as well as the people who lost faith in him. He wanted that more than anything; not even his vendetta against Texas Tech was equitable to peace. He squirmed, looking beyond the champagne popping of the cheerful women and lifestyle that consumed him. He knew Samantha was on her way back to Colorado. He knew his father was in the ground, wondering if he had anything to inherit from the will. It was worth holding on to a whim. With one swooping motion, he snatched the paper and tore it into two; the mortified face of Lars appearing through the schism.

"I'm done here, Lars.

"But...you can't! I mean, you *can* but this was so close to being sealed. I was going to be your partner and all. The best damn defense since Johnny Cochran and O.J."

"No, *done*."

Jeff passed by the party and out of the cafe. He knew he made the right choice, for as he looked over his shoulder, he bore witness to Lars cozying up to a bridesmaid immediately afterward. He was a fraud and untrustworthy, just like himself, but no more. Jeff returned home to a lightless home with a jam-packed mailbox. It contained a letter from the landlord, begging for him or Samantha to contact them before an eviction was instated. It also contained past-due utilities, membership cancellations, and one thick letter from an attorney, but not a malicious one, an ally. Jeff pried the corners open and revealed a lengthy, yet revolutionary text. Despite his decaying family bonds, his father's will remain unchanged. He was receiving a portion of the life insurance! Jeff jumped, banging his head on the lamp, and raided the fridge. He downed an entire bottle of water.

"Let's get it done!"

He hopped on his computer and refunded every single book order that night. He made amends with the irate customers, diffusing any more pending lawsuits. His livid generosity mimicked that of a found again Ebenezer Scrooge. He made sure that Pollination Station was to be disbanded forever, gone without a trace as soon as all the orders were closed.

He felt an immense fluttering in his chest as if his heart was fracturing a calcified cocoon and pounding once again. His fingers were ablaze. Sweat dripped and plopped onto the desk. In the blink of an eye, all his authors' books vanished into the ether. He blacklisted Lars, his printer, and his various editors and publicists that did absolutely nothing for him. They were ghosts that have been plasticized and formed into his new fantasy: a non-profit literary journal. He sighed, pushing back from the desk and the thousands of emails that were answered. Not one was overlooked, not one was unaddressed, aside from one. He scrolled down his phone, fumigated from the leeches and gold diggers and, upon the 4th entry, clicked the name. The phone rang and rang. On the last ring, Samantha picked up. Jeff grinned from the other end. If only she could see the benevolence he channeled.

"What the hell do you want?"

"It's done. *All* done. Everything will go back to normal, I promise."

***

Samantha was about to check out when Jeff called her. She was on the last $50 bill she owned, which was going to go directly into her gas tank. Colorado called for her as well, but she took Jeff's call.

"You are, huh? You won't end up in a prison jumpsuit?" Samantha said.

"Not this guy. Sam, babe, I've changed. I'm through with this materialistic scrap heap I called a life. I'm burnt."

"But, Jeff. You cheated on me with some skank. God knows how many sloppy blowjobs you've gotten by your fucking hookers either!"

The line went silent.

"No, I did *not* solicit! You know me by now with casual sex. If *anyone* was to do that, it was Ethan Lane."

"I don't know who the fuck he is, but it doesn't exonerate you."

"I swear, Sam, you got to be—"

"So, you gonna' tell me where you got all the money?"

"It was," Jeff pulled the phone away to stifle some tears. "My father. Turns out, he didn't write me out of the will. I guess he had a heart."

"What an unlikely, yet fortunate, turn of events." Samantha felt sympathy flowing through the phone line. She couldn't fully trust him, but the tone of his exasperated voice told her plenty more.

"All the people are refunded. I got ahold of the landlord. There will be money to bring the place back to normal, hell, I can put a down payment on a damn house. For us. Or, take these student loans and shove them down the gullet of Sallie *and* Mae. This time, I will do it right."

"You grew your hair back out again, didn't you?"

"Yes."

"Ah, Jeffrey. Glad to hear you're on the come around."

"Where are you?"

"15 miles from Santa Fe," Samantha said, a lush inflection of the 'e' drifted into Jeff's ear. "Motel 6, by the Target. 3rd floor."

***

Jeff arrived in under a half hour. His car tires omitted an acrid smell of abuse. He jettisoned up the stairs, bypassed the confused clerk, and pounded the elevator key. Once on her floor, he strutted to her room, sweating, with a bouquet of roses. She opened the door, eyeing up her estranged boyfriend in all his flannel and ripped denim glory. He stepped inside and handed her the flowers.

"Mhm they smell nice," Samantha said, eyeing him up. "You look very, Jeffrey-esque. Come closer."

"I like that term," Jeff said, a smug sparkle in his eye. "Did you just come up with that?"

When he was in range, Samantha delivered a swift arching kick to his groin. He collapsed forward, bemoaning, and wept.

"Was *that* witty enough? You're lucky you never fucked your 'bae' or your cock would be smithereens."

Jeff lumbered up, his face alight like a cherry. He was wheezing.

"You...are a saint."

"I told you I was like this from the start, Jeff. I hope you didn't sell all my shit."

"I promise."

"Good!"

Samantha leapt onto the bed and flicked on the television. "I have an hour before check-out and I sure as hell am going to use it."

Jeff made his way to a chair and opened the mini-fridge. A bottle of water was calling his name. They sat in silence, save for Jerry Springer reruns. A young couple was arguing over who had custody of their five children. The man, ironically, looked like Jeff, which made Samantha giggle.

"See? At least you're not like this sucker. You have a brain and can keep your cock on a leash, I hope."

A twang of pain made Jeff wince, but he eventually laughed as his caricature tossed over the cheap plywood table. Black-shirted security guards surrounded him. His face was also cherry, but out of anger.

***

Jeff helped Samantha pack up and they blazed down the New Mexico highway. Jeff, with his sleeves, rolled up, Samantha with her bare feet out the window. His Volvo was still kicking, despite a sooty diesel exhaust cloud occasionally protruding from the rear. Samantha was on her phone.

"Fucking Glanceagram, man," she said. "I found so many recipes and hot yoga goths to gawk over. Now, I decided to cancel it. I'm glad to see you did as well."

"Well, of course," Jeff said. "If the people have any complaints still, they can email me. So far, nothing."

"I did see one thing though and it looks pretty fucking stupid."

"What?"

"This 'poet', Tyler Young, is having some kind of reading in Lubbock, Texas tomorrow. Saw it in some ad."

"Oh, fuck that guy! He got famous by luck, pure luck. You may call my old press trite and hippy, but this guy? He's the epitome of 'insta-fame'. I bet he paid for all his followers."

Samantha turned to Jeff, a devious grin spread on her face.

"You feel what I'm feeling?

Jeff flicked his turn signal for the next exit. Their apartment was near.

"I wouldn't miss it for the world."

***

Ethan Lane sat in his latest fan girl's apartment somewhere in Kansas. He took off his noise-canceling headphones, that earlier had blocked out everything, except the latest indie band to grace the chart. He was reflecting on the week's events as he jotted in a journal. Jeff never delivered on the promises of the publishing contract. There was no distribution in major retailers or the promise of more poetry books to come. He felt like a fraud pandering to the lowest common denominator on his Glanceagram page. Ethan wanted nothing more than to write thought-provoking poetry, but he understood what his mindless followers wanted.

Ethan scrolled on Barney&Jules.com to look at Tyler's book sales. *Dirty Panties and Pelagius* was in the top 5 overall, yet there were hundreds of bad reviews. Granted, there were thousands overall, but it was unsettling. He then typed in his book, *Everlong Lust*, and saw that it was not only still for sale, but it ranked in the hundreds of thousands. Nothing shy of relevant. He sighed and messaged Tyler Young. He wasn't expecting Tyler to reply to him on Glanceagram, but he was pleasantly surprised to see the familiar ellipses pop up. The message read:

St. Augustine shall hath his revenge'

"I must know more!" Ethan said. He scrolled down and saw Lubbock, TX was the start of his 'Costumed Poetry Tour' and knew he had a chance to make it if he left first thing in the morning. He texted Baefore and After—since he was too anxious to go to her room.

Prepare my case dove. I leave tomorrow xoxo

Twenty-four

Julie left the podium with much fanfare from the esteemed audience. She sat down in the front row and Waters stood up. He was cooled off but kept a handkerchief in his breast pocket.

"Julie! That was a...wonderful speech. Take notes, Ivy League." He laughed, seeing only rustling in the back.

"Guns up!" Patricia yelled. "By the way, and I must say for all of us, dis here shrimp is fresh and ripe. Good lookin', chef."

"Ok then. Thank you...ma'am. Now, I must say this banquet didn't turn out so bad, once we got the air patched up and—"

Chancellor Rails stepped in, making the door creak. He slid through with his phone clenched at the waist.

"Ah, Chancellor! So glad to see you. Welcome."

Rails sat in the back, rigid. He didn't say a word, despite his VIP list sitting to his right.

"Ok then, let's begin the slide-show, shall we? Our magnificent English department set this up for our prestigious guests. Afterward, bestselling author and MFA candidate, River Chang, will close out with a reading."

A light applause followed.

"All I need to do is click this," Waters squinted at the small screen embedded within the podium. "This little icon…perfect!"

The video began in black & white with a panning out of the marching band playing the school anthem. Everyone but Waters was staring at something other than the projector screen. The occasional hoot from Ray or Patricia whisked through. Leroy was passed out in a chair with his head back and snoring. Suzie was exploring the admin building unattended.

"We welcome you to Texas Tech," a young Chancellor Rails said. He was standing in front of the landmark statue at the entrance, the "Masked Raider". He had significantly more black hair than he did presently.

"There is much for you to see, including our famous statue, Masked Raider." Rails' lips were pursed, yet Dr. Weaver could hear growling. The video then cut to color and a modern campus appeared with hip students walking around and socializing. There was even a shot of Chang's lecture—thankfully, before Jeff intruded—which brought him to tears. Julie touched his leg, knowing how traumatized he was from the event. Then, as soon as Julie appeared to introduce the English department, the video stopped and a circular 'Waiting' text popped up.

"What in tarnation is going on?" Waters said. He pushed some buttons to no avail. "Well, this is embarrassing. It should be ready to go in no ti—"

The screen went black, then cut to a small brothel room with an attractive woman in lingerie sprawled on the bed. Waters' face went pale.

"Oh, this is totally not right," he said, pressing multiple buttons to minimize the video, but it was too late. The door opened and there he was, wearing only a towel around his thick waist. A lump in the front set the precedent.

"Oh, dear lord!" Doctor Weaver shouted, covering her eyes. Many more appalled gasps echoed through the hall. Julie and Chang shrieked.

"I…I can explain!" Waters stammered. He was now undressing the woman. His towel fell off.

"By golly, boss!" Patricia said to Lester. "I know that fella. Hardly believed I ain't notice sooner." Patricia locked eyes with Waters and blew a kiss. "I'll see you lata', muffin."

Waters tried to at least turn down the volume but hit the wrong lever. Sounds of sex filled the hall at a decibel level no one ever wanted to hear.

"Turn that shit off right now!" a voice protruded.

"I'm trying, I'm trying!" Waters screamed. He fingered for the plug and yanked it out before the conclusion. Lester booed.

"Waters! You are a true sum'bitch." Rails called out from the back. "Not only do you butcher this prized banquet, but *someone* passed around this muck like hot cakes…to everyone."

"Like…who?"

"The entire English department…and many others. I'm done with your rotten ass. You're fired, you moron. Right here, right now!"

Waters fainted, hitting the ground hard with his stomach. Many guests exited the banquet hall chatting a frenzy. Julie hid her face in her hands; blackened eyeliner tears smudged her face. Suddenly, an echo of tire screeches caught the attention of the crowd.

"Now what?" Rails said, stomping to the window. Julie and Chang scurried over as well, noticing a large SUV spinning recklessly around the parking lots and grounds. The lush grass was marred by deep brown ruts.

"It's heading to the statue!" Chang said.

Rails looked on as the vehicle began doing donuts around his cherished cornerstone; the flowers were shredded and flung all over. He slammed his phone to the ground, shattering it.

"Why? Just, why?" he said.

Julie frowned as the vehicle looped around the statue for the last time and sped off into the hazy Texas horizon. She, of all people, knew who the culprit was, the only man on the planet that would stop at nothing to ruin Texas Tech and even her own life. She put a hand on her abdomen and felt an unusual panging.

Why? Just, why?" she whispered.

Rails threw a tantrum. He toppled the podium, destroying the microphone and soundboard, and pulled down the fabric banner from the wall and stomped on it.

"Why…did…this…happen?" He screamed.

"Where's Mag?" Suzie said at the entrance.

"Chancellor Rails, please calm down," Julie said. "We can still continue…right?"

She looked at the banquet hall; nearly everyone had vacated. Chang was still seated, weeping.

"Oh, what did I do to deserve this hell?" he said.

"River," Julie said.

As Julie picked up her papers, she was approached by Doctor Weaver and Professor Teuton.

"Oh, Doctor….and professor," she stuttered. "I'm so sorry that—"

"Ms. Pinner, please," Doctor Weaver said, resting her hand on her tense shoulder. "This was not of your doing. You just did what you were meant to do and to be honest, we enjoyed your speech, right Teuton?" She looked over at the staggering professor. He burped.

"Why, yes, we do, *a lot.*"

Julie smiled. "I'm so glad."

Doctor Weaver leaned in close to Julie's ear. "And to be honest, we weren't even looking forward to Mr. Chang. We only have one scholarship to give today and we want to give it to you."

Julie dropped her papers. Her jaw went slack.

"Are you...serious?"

"Absolutely," Doctor Weaver beamed. We can sign the paperwork in the lobby. We'd love to see you in Philadelphia this August."

Julie internalized the good news. She stood silent. Her pupils enlarged. She shrieked in joy and hugged Doctor Weaver.

"This is a dream come true. Thank you, thank you thank you!"

"Come, now," Doctor Weaver said, motioning her to follow.

"Wait, can I join? I wish to read you my haikus!" Chang said as he noticed the trio exiting.

"We, uh, decided to look for other candidates. I'm sorry," Doctor Weaver said.

"Yeah, you heard the lady. Shove on off you little prick!" Lester said from the back. Chang shivered, lost his balance, and fainted in his chair.

"Mista' Ray! The po' boy. Watch that tongue of yours!" Patricia scolded.

"I say, this bourbon has gotten me off my rocker!" Ray said in jest. "C'mon Y'all. Let's get out of this joint b'fore the Chancellor come on back with a 12 gauge!"

The group tramped out, leaving Leroy still snoring in the chair. No one dared to wake him.

***

As Max sped off the campus forever, leaving all four phases for Texas Tech to clean up, he patted the treatise on the passenger seat.

"Perhaps, I'm unaware of the full consequences of my devious plan, yet I could hear St. Francis of Assisi rejoice in the heavens. My final act of revenge caused the pigeons on campus to collectively migrate to a better home, somewhere far away from the doldrums of Lubbock."

Max thought while pointing in the direction of El Rito, New Mexico. He had it all planned out. He would stay with his sister until Paul Garrett could organize everything for his poetry tour. Paul was more than happy to handle everything since Max's book sales were steady and money was no longer an issue for the press. Max swindled his followers on Glanceagram into buying his real poetry book, which caused an influx of bad reviews, but at the same time, much curiosity.

"Mindless sheep will get a taste of my real craft and not know whether my virtual alter ego, Tyler Young, is real or…me. Oh, what a conundrum for their peon brains. The wisdom of St. Benedict and his rule of law hath now fallen on the plains of West Texas. Judgment comes quickly upon the heathens! Is it only just my Opus Dei?"

Max laughed, even more, tantalizing his brain. Even his own theology was becoming warped. Professor Anderson planted the seed to reveal the duality of man. It was all so clear to him now; Max was the living embodiment of a modern-day crusader, albeit with the purpose of preserving upstanding literature. The ghosts of Longfellow and Yeats would be his guide on his divine providence poetry tour.

"Those who are lost shall hear my voice crying in the wilderness! I alone can convert them from this pop poetry pandemic! Let Romanticism be my guide! There is still hope for mankind and his inherent goodness!" Max said while he stomped the gas. His SUV rumbled forward, burping with the flood of gasoline to the engine. He was a madman, weaving around cars in straightaways. Occasionally, his blading tires would graze the shoulder, flinging up dust in front of other drivers. It was only then when Max remembered. He gasped, jerking the SUV out of the center stripe.

"But, what about…Augustine?"

Twenty-five

Chancellor Rails pulled his black Lexus into the driveway; his mansion was the envy of the gated community. Rails shuttered to think what the newspaper's headline might be in the morning. The possibilities were endless: "Sex Scandal at Tech!", "Prostitution Ring: Dean and Chancellor Implicated", "Fresh Pleasure: Tech Financing Smut Motel?" There was little left to the imagination and Rails was not having it. At least he eliminated the diseased leaf of Waters. Maybe that was all that needed to happen.

"Where has your ass been?" Linda Rails greeted her husband in the kitchen, with her hands on her hips. "You entertaining some tramp at the awards banquet? I bet it was a night to remember," Linda scowled.

"Let's not talk about it. I'm exhausted and want to go to bed," Rails said.

"And I suppose you know one of your deans is all over the internet frolicking with some stranger from China?"

"That's preposterous and you know it. You can believe everything you see floating around cyberspace," the Chancellor replied, lying through his teeth.

"I'm sure your dean—do I dare identify him as—Dean Waters? He isn't the only one to struggle with infidelity," Linda snapped.

"Aren't you a hypocrite? I'm going to bed!" Rails screamed.

"Keep your voice down! You might wake up your daughter, Kasey. Do you even remember her? You and she might spend some quality time together since you seem to have no role in her life."

"Shut up, you old bag. Just do your exercise and spend some more of my money."

Kasey Rails jolted to the kitchen as her parents continued to berate one another. She was weeping.

"There's your daughter now and she's more than upset with you. Her tears are not for me that's for sure," Linda said as she walked over to console her only daughter, who Rails speculated was not his since she didn't resemble him. He would tell the neighbors she's a splitting image.

"It's alright honey. I want to make it up to you. Maybe we can go shopping tomorrow," Rails said approaching Kasey with a lumbered benevolence.

"Quit trying to buy her love, you moron. There's nothing you can do to make amends for your years of neglect, but it would be good for you two to spend some time together as I mentioned earlier." She turned to Kasey, stooping down a bit. "Would you like that precious?"

Kasey sobbed an Oscar performance but didn't say anything.

"Surely, there is something you and your father might enjoy. Don't you like that poet? Didn't you tell me he is giving a reading at Barney & Jules next week? What is his name? Is it Taylor something?"

Kasey lifted her head from her hands and wiped the tears from her eyes. "His name is Tyler Young and yes I want to see him. All my friends will be there too."

"That settles it then. Your father will take you to see him next week. Isn't that right, Henry?"

"That sounds like a splendid idea. We'll make a date of it. Now if you'll both excuse me, I'm going to bed."

Kasey began to cry again and buried her face in her mother's chest.

"What is it now sweetie?" Linda asked.

"I ordered Tyler's book and…it's not here yet!"

"Everything will be alright. I'm sure it will come in the mail soon." Linda patted her daughter's head, thinking about how to take her husband for every cent.

***

Susan Wilson grew up as the protective big sister of Max. She had to watch out for her little brother because he had a penchant for chicanery from a young age. When she saw his beat-up SUV roll into the driveway, she was outside, helping him with his possessions.

"Oh, Max. So, so nice to see you again." Susan said, giving him a hug. He dwarfed her in size, so she always had to step on her tiptoes to embrace him.

"My beloved sister, I am forever grateful for your hospitality. I can assure you my visit will be short lived as I have a divine calling ahead."

"Ah, there you go with your enigmas again," Susan laughed. "I suppose we have much to catch up on?"

They took Max's things to the living room. There wasn't much, but they were heavy bags—for her at least.

"Come, now. I have some fresh lemonade for you. Would you like a sandwich? I made muffulettas the other day and have a craving for more."

"Sure. I could use a filling meal before I ascend to heaven."

They ate and drank, catching up on familiar things.

"I had to check mom back into rehab again."

"Oh, what in the world did she do now?" Max said, downing a huge portion of lemonade.

"Kept yelling again. At everything, from the squirrels to the children. Had the police do a welfare check and she punched one. She'll be in for two weeks."

"That explains all the Boone's Farm. By the way, do you have any Rolling Rock?"

"No, silly. You know I don't drink." She turned to face him. "So, what made you drop out? You know that this town was rooting for you."

"I can't get into my reasoning for my foresight into the failure of academia right now, but rest assured through much prayer and supplication, I made the right decision. It wasn't easy to reach this conclusion, for weeks I lay in bed with nothing but sackcloth on and ashes smeared on my body. My repentance cleared my faculties, allowing me to be of sound mind. I'm done with the literary cesspool known as Texas Tech."

"Sounds like nonsense to me, with you so close to graduating."

"Sometimes we must be like the sparrow and let the Lord provide. I suppose you have been slaving away in the kitchen, preparing a celebratory meal for your brother's return?"

She spat in the sink. "You can heat up a burrito in the microwave. And what's this business about a poetry tour? I never knew you wrote poetry."

"I haven't been writing it lately, mainly jotting down some trite universal dung on my phone, to the delight of teen and tween girls everywhere."

"What *exactly* have you been doing, Max?"

"I, your brother, have become a global sensation, but I can't get into the specifics now. My publisher, Paul Garrett, has set up this poetry tour, which is sure to leave my fans thrilled and rigid with excitement. I do need your help, however, in the spirit of Carnivale, I need a costume for my poetic performances."

"A costume? For what? Do you plan on embarrassing yourself in front of whoever might show up at your little poetry reading?"

"Don't jest, sister, this is of the utmost importance. Unfortunately, the tour commences back in Lubbock. I didn't want to return to Hades so soon, but as I mentioned, my publisher is handling such affairs."

"There's plenty of clothes in my bedroom closet. You're sure to find a costume there."

Max didn't hesitate and rummaged for the Holy Grail of costumes. It would be vital to have a disguise, to add a sense of mystery and flair. Nothing immediately caught his attention, but among the tides of neutral pastels, he spotted a pink feather boa nestled in the back of the closet. "Oh, ho ho. The grail indeed." Max wrapped the boa around his neck and stared at himself in the mirror.

He rustled some more and found a blond wig and pair of dark sunglasses to complete his outfit. "Now, *this*. This is a joy." His transformation into Tyler Young right then and there and couldn't get enough. He cackled with laughter, which made Susan perk up.

"Heavens, I hope he didn't just find my toys…"

Twenty-six

Max's phone rang, disturbing his early morning slumber.

"Hey man!" Paul Garrett shouted, making Max retract the phone. "You ready for tonight? I'm sorry I can't make it but you know I have a real job. But I took care of everything...sent some posters that had your Glanceagram profile pic...I can't believe you told me about this shit not that long ago...this poetry tour...man...it's killer!"

"Calm down. I told you we were going to see some sales...and yes, the worthless poetry medium Glanceagram is the reason why and don't worry. I'll be in Lubbock soon." Max groaned. Paul Garrett was but a pawn in his game.

"No need…you wait for us. I got another surprise…a limo will pick you up and take you to Barney & Jules. I told them to pick you up at Bledsoe Hall at six-thirty...want you to arrive in style...don't be late, man."

"I'm not in Tech anymore. In New Mexico with family."

"Oh…that wasn't mentioned," Paul Garrett said disdainfully.

"Well, it'll have to do. I'll text you the address."

"Ok. Anyways, anything else you need, champ?"

Max rubbed his chin. "A limo. I suppose that will add to my grand entrance. I won't be late…and as for my costume it's sure to leave my audience speechless…it's part glam rock star…part hipster and the wig adds credibility of course."

"I hear the place is sold out and better yet it's twenty bucks a head. We're cleaning their clocks tonight." Paul said.

"Wait…you're charging them? I've never heard of that. I don't know any famous writer, much less a poet, that does that…it seems the epitome of greed—" Max could feel the moral fibers snapping. "—if they're willing to pay, then all is fair in love and shit poetry."

"You're a star! What are you reading? Something from that pop poetry book you mentioned?"

"Let me handle the selection of poems. I must be going. Gonna bathe. Thank you, dear publisher."

Max laughed, hung up, and faceplanted back into the pillow.

***

Dean Waters sat in his condo with his possessions from his office. For the first time in his esteemed career, he was fired, and Chancellor Rails was raining down his fury on him. Pensions were up in the air. He was questioned by university lawyers to diffuse any conspiracies from the press. His actions at the Barry Motel were haphazard and infused with impulse, and it didn't help he would visit on company time and with his business credit card.

"I'm so fucking stupid," he moaned.

There was really nothing he could do to weasel out of it. He was caught up in the legalities and the university was exhausting their options. Who would hire him after this? His legacy would be tarnished, but even more so if he faced jail time. He was sweating like a pig, wishing he had an escape.

"Never in a million years, would he have thought the Barry Motel savvy enough to have cameras. I've been going there for years."

Waters paced around, with one hand on his bourbon bottle, the other on his hip. Taking a few swigs, he reached into a desk drawer and found the pistol. This was it. No Ivy League dreams, no chance at redemption. Waters placed the gun to his temple and put his finger on the trigger.

"I got my gun up alright," he said, sardonically. His forehead wrinkled, lips quivering. He pulled, but nothing. The gun jammed.

"My God!" he said. "No, I want this to resolve. *I want* to live!"

He put down the weapons of mass destruction and hopped on his computer. Deleting his browser history and bookmarks of all his porn, he replaced them with his resume, real estate brokers, and colleges with vacancies. He scoured the country for a place where nobody knew him and remote enough to bury his past.

"Hmm," he said. "English professor position available at Northern New Mexico Community College in El Rito. A place with a bright future!"

He sent in his resume, lit a cigar, and opened the window. He knew Texas wouldn't miss him.

***

Ethan Lane drove his Toyota Camry through Roscoe, TX. It had been a long trip from Venice Beach, but he broke it up by staying with fangirls in Phoenix and Albuquerque. It was the norm, and playing the sap certainly garnished him a free stay, if not more pleasantries. He stopped to get gas and got some uncomfortable stares from a few locals, one of which told him, 'to get his long-haired ass back to California.' Ethan shrugged it off with a muted chuckle and left, fearing a double-barrel shotgun to be trailing him.

With some luck, Ethan hoped to talk with Tyler about how he had maintained his Glanceagram popularity. Lately, Ethan hadn't been getting as much love on his page, since he was taking a hiatus and in tow, some followers disappeared. He knew that very few would even care about his poetry if he wasn't on these social media platforms. Ironically, they seemed to leave him feeling alone and it all seemed too much to handle. The pop poet glancers were a fickle bunch at best and Ethan could only recycle the same she-quote so many times. He played himself out and thought if anyone knew how to revitalize his Glanceagram page, it would be Tyler Young.

There were times when Ethan wanted to delete his Glanceagram page altogether and become a real poet. He even thought of submitting his work to some literary journals He sent scores of emails with hardly a reputable cover letter, which was always returned negatively. Ethan found himself stuck in a mire of mediocrity; giving what his followers wanted was the last thing he desired. However, it didn't take away from his hardline/softline stock of coffee mugs and hoodies. The icing on the cake being several teenage girls posting pictures of "the moon is her lover" mugs. With Jeff leaving him high and dry, this was the only way to stay afloat. The real tragedy was that he was a living contradiction.

Twenty-seven

Ethan Lane arrived at the Barney & Jules in Lubbock, TX to see a line wrapped around the store. It consisted of mainly teen and tween girls and their listless parents that didn't know exactly why they were there.

Ethan felt out of place until a few teen girls came rushing up to him.

"Are you Ethan Lane the poet?" one girl asked.

"Yes, I am, how did you know?" Ethan blushed. To think, someone would recognize him all the way out in Lubbock, TX.

"We all follow you on Glanceagram. We *love* your poetry!" the girl said, elated.

"Can you follow us back?" One looked dreamily into Ethan's eyes. It was a way of asking for an autograph.

"Sure, what is your handle?" Ethan smiled, candidly, pondering if it was smart for a grown man to follow a teenage girl.

"Oh my god! Ethan Lane followed us!"

As the name Ethan Lane broke out among the crowd, many more people of all genders flocked. It was a paparazzi of smartphone cameras and outreached hands just looking to grace a sliver of his worn-out cardigan. After what seemed like fifteen minutes of fame for Ethan, it all ended when the black limo pulled up.

"That's him! That's Tyler Young! Oh my God! That's really him!"

With a clink of the door handle, a plume of dry ice blew from the cabin. His entourage, donned in suits, was immediately swarmed with fanatics. Max arose as Tyler Young. The pink feather boa wrapped around his fat neck, the blond wig whipping in the breeze, the dark shades clinging to his swollen head. Once the fog cleared, there was a queer silence. Muted gabbling began to spread.

"Wait, is that him? *That's* Tyler Young? He's nothing like his profile pic." a young woman said.

"Ew, he looks sweaty…and drunk," a boy said, combing his faded hair with his fingers.

Max strutted out of the limo like Tiberius after throwing a few senators off a cliff. He flipped the pink boa over his left shoulder as if being knighted by Queen Victoria. He had to play the part to give his fans what they wanted.

"Sup broheims? I'm Tyler Young, alright. Sorry. Just came from a banger in Portland. Lots of beer and vapes, real facts. Who wants a signed copy of my book? I sign with reclaimed maple sap."

The crowd, which was completely clueless at first, immediately switched gears and became ecstatic.

"Oh, I want one!"

"Ah! Me, too!"

"Oh, what mindless swine," Max thought while carrying *Dirty Panties and Pelagius.* A bodyguard was chucking books into the crowd. Some goers were even scrapping over copies, tearing the book in half and demanding a replacement. The older crowd just looked onward, squinting at the spectacle; the man that was taking their money right from their back pockets.

"If it's a reading they want, then I shall oblige. Oh, by the way, these books are $49.99 each. My boys will be around to collect," Max said, walking through the front door.

The bookstore was packed with more of the same crowd; some shoddy housewives and downtrodden men from the corner store evened it out. Max trotted towards the stage hearing snickers from a few girls, "What the fuck? Where's Tyler?"

"Bunch of potty-mouthed wenches, Satan loves sassy tarts! Am I right?" He shouted into the crowd, many applauded. All it took was some boisterous comments to offset the negativity. Behind him, two giant posters of 'Tyler Young' flanked him. It was a model, of course, flexing a dilapidated bicep adorned with tribal tattoos. He had a beard, with a beanie. His ice-blue eyes gazed upon the oddly complacent audience.

Suddenly, a star struck Ethan Lane stepped in front of him.

"Oh, wow! Tyler Young. I'm Ethan Lane. Nice to mee—"

"Out of my way, you ignorant ragamuffin!" Max said, casting the fragile Ethan away. A chair managed to contain him from slamming onto the tile.

The crowd gasped but was broken up by some fierce bravado from the boys. Some parents corralled their children and headed out the door. The manager of Barney & Jules did a brief introduction that no one paid attention to. Max was getting annoyed.

"My children! Why do you depart from my gospel? The show is about to begin!"

People from the outside assumed the empty seats. More fans cheered and clapped.

"Veni, Vidi, Vici, my distinguished glancers and literary critics alike. Tonight, I shall commence my reading with selected poems, from my beloved chapbook, *Dirty Panties, and Pelagius.* I know many of you have gotten a signed copy outside." As nearly on cue, the large bodyguards began circling the crowd, card readers in hand to collect. The crowd grew silent and attentive, for the most part; some grumbled detests rose as they shelled out their wares.

Max lifted his head, catching beams of light on the dark sunglasses. He looked like clergyman in drag. He noticed that more people were leaving without refilling or paying. But, in the back corner, he was able to make out Chancellor Rails. The last person he expected to be here, underneath his towering presence. Max grinned, knowing that Rails, just hours earlier, experienced the worst moment in his career—and possibly his entire life. Even he could captivate his sworn enemies with such grandeur and posterity. He couldn't hold back. He laughed, causing a disturbance in the crowd. 'Why is he laughing?' a few people noted, until Max slammed his fist on the podium, silencing the crowd like Augustus Caesar with a hangover.

"Hark, heathens! Hath not the age of St. Augustine swept to victory from the jaws of defeat? Did not Pelagius fail? Were not his fruits of labor in vain? I stand before your peon minds as your savior tonight. Weren't you yet sinners crying out in the wilderness? Awaiting the one who would prepare the way for the Messiah? Am I *not* great? For I am your humble servant Tyler. My morphisms have brightened your day and my triteness hath fed your soul upon the glowing screen. Fear, not my children! Though the end is near, we shall not weaken our iron will to overcome this great sin committed against us ...this injustice is here tonight." Max belched. "Oh, angels trumpet, swoon."

Kasey Rails, who was tucked away near the children's section, began to cry and buried her face in her hands, "I wanted to see Tyler…not whatever the fuck he is! I want to go home now, Daddy!"

The Chancellor felt his heart flutter, it was the first time anyone had called him "Daddy". However, his arms throbbed.

"This is an outrage! Excuse me, where is the manager?" Rails asked a woman in a Barney & Jules uniform. Max continued to drone in the background.

"I want my money back, goddammit!"

"Calm down sir, there are no refunds. I can have security escort you out if you don't get out of my face," the angsty employee said.

"That won't be necessary, we are leaving right, Kasey? And don't touch me or I'll sue. And you don't know who I am? I'm the Chancellor of Texas Tech!"

Within seconds, the bodyguards were upon him.

"Sir, did you pay for your signed copy?"

"No, why the hell—oh, I mean, yes! Your other associate took my money." Rails stuttered, pointing at a random person in the crowd.

"I don't buy it. Give me the damn book."

"Excuse me? I am Chancellor of Texas Tech! Do not speak profanities in front of my daughter, you bastard!"

The opposing man performed a full nelson on Rails, creaking his weary bones. "Ow, ow!" he wailed as and was forced out; Kasey shortly behind carrying only the signed page of Tyler's chapbook.

***

Jeff and Samantha pulled up to the parking lot of Barney & Jules. They found a mid-way parking space after seeing some people leaving the store.

"So, this is Tyler Young's crowd? Seems pretty packed!" Samantha said.

"I'll believe it when I see it," Jeff replied, staring into the rearview to look at his hair.

"You're still checking on that ol' mop of yours?" Samantha said, laughing.

"Hush, now."

"C'mon. Let's go see the 'spectacle' himself."

They got out and walked, hand in hand, to the front door. Scores of young fans were reading some of the work aloud from chapbooks. Some cooed, some cursed aloud as if the work itself truly divided all who read it. Three teenage girls took a selfie in front of a Tyler Young poster in the window. Jeff and Samantha took their place to stare at the being.

"Quite larger than life, huh?" Samantha said.

"He…he looks like how I did," Jeff said.

His stomach ached; triggered memories of long nights at clubs with other peoples' money began swirling in his head. It made his fibrous heartthrob with a new kind of force, a force of vivacious reckoning that was prophesized for millennia. He continued to stare at the poster while his upper lip quivered. Samantha, after staring at his deconstructing moment, nudged his side.

"Babe, don't take it so seriously," she reassured.

"Yes, yes of course. Sorry, just had a moment there." She felt her hands slide up his arm.

"Let's go. We both need a laugh."

Inside, a slogging lecture, with a vocabulary that Jeff hadn't heard since freshman year, bewitched the mystified crowd. In the corner, Chancellor Rails was prostrate on the ground with a knee to his neck and under restraints. "Yo! That's my old chancellor. What the fuck is going on?" Jeff said, gawking at the sight. Moans quickly dissipated once the fiasco ended; the turned heads turned back to the presenter. Samantha sat in the middle, flanked by two teenage girls with hands clasped and silent tears trickling down their faces. Jeff squeezed around and gazed upon the ludicrous sight that was Tyler Young.

"Is this the opening act? Looks nothing like the poster," Samantha whispered.

"Who knows," Jeff retorted, unamused.

The reading continued, and Jeff grew annoyed, quivering his lip again. He swore that 'Pelagius' was spoken every other line. It mimicked his outburst at Texas Tech, with a pretentious River Chang droning on and on about nonsensical hopes and dreams of the budding writer. As Tyler closed his book, the audience erupted in a grand applause; some called for an encore. Jeff contemplated a retort by lowering his head and Samantha sensed that something was wrong.

"Jeff?" She asked, timidly, stroking his arm.

"I'm gonna do it—"

"No, please not again."

"Stop this nonsense!" he yelled. The room all stared at him. Max, who was infatuated with his power, searched the room behind his sunglasses.

"Who dares interrupt my sermon? Waif! Identify yourself."

"My identity and name are unimportant. Are you this great Tyler Young that everyone is ogling over? You look like Ignatius Reilly fell into a pile of clothes at a sex shop." Only Samantha giggled; the crowd looked confused.

"An ignoramus I see…Yes, I am, your savior. The age of Pelagius is nigh, and you will not prevent the reckoning from absorbing you all."

Jeff, who was seething, finally rose. The disapproval of the audience rose with him, some booing the scene.

"You sound an awful lot like someone I used to know." Jeff inquired. He scrutinized the pink boa and blonde hair, perusing through his mind's catalog of whose face was supported by that swollen neck. He shuffled to the end, despite Samantha hissing at him to rescind. As Jeff strutted closer to the stage, Max started shivering. It was Jeff, his old friend, now accosting him and the ruse that took an eternity to devise and execute. He wasn't willing to give it up so easily. The boa felt tighter around his throat.

"Uh, you do not need to come up here...hey, where's security? We have a situation!" Max stuttered.

"Hey, Jeff! Remember me?" A voice emitted from stage right: it was Ethan Lane. Jeff froze in place.

"Oh, yes, hi. Glad to see you again."

"What you did wasn't cool, man. Like really. I had all these fans waiting for the book," He waved his arms out to the crows. "And you didn't even make it, man."

"I rectified it with a refund, *man*," Jeff snapped back. His snide attitude was brimming.

"Hey, uh, I ordered a book and haven't gotten it yet," A person said.

"Stay out of this!" Jeff commanded.

"And don't you talk to Tyler like that. He did nothing to you, man. Let him read. We all love him."

"He speaks of dogma and false praise. Are you that brain-dead that you can't read the lies spewing forth?"

"The only liar here is you, man," Ethan said. He encroached Jeff, drawing 'ooo's' from the crowd. Max stepped backward from the podium, texting a million miles an hour, looking for an escape. Ethan glared at Jeff with his doe-eyed innocence, yet Jeff could feel his anger exuding from within. Samantha remained motionless in the crowd; her teeth clenched behind pursed lips.

"Look. I did the best I could and failed. You got your money back. Go and self-publish if you want. It's not that hard."

Ethan stepped closer, nearly six inches away. The audience rustled. One person yelled, "You won't hit him!" and another even said, "Kiss and make up!" It was yet another bizarre and divisive moment. Max, who was now off the raised stage, knelt below, calling Paul Garrett for assistance, yet the call went to voicemail every time. Still no sign of security. In an instant, a collective shriek erupted and Max turned around to witness Jeff and Ethan brawling on the floor. "Holy shit," Max said and retreated into the thick of the shelves. Samantha, now hovering over her boyfriend, attempted to pry Jeff off the busted pulp that was becoming Ethan Lane.

"Jeff! Fucking stop it! You're going to get arrested," Samantha said.

"Not…until…he says…he's sorry!" Jeff said, exasperated. Ethan was able to wriggle free and deliver a kick to Jeff's stomach, rendering him coughing on the floor for a moment. Ethan scrambled to his feet but was drugged down again by Jeff's outreached hand. The two continued to brawl and the crowd formed a circle around them. Chairs were scattered all over the place. Barney & Jules staff alerted the security, who were smoking cigarettes outside after deferring Rails, and darted in. Careless cigarettes were flung from their mouths and hands onto the salesfloor unnoticed.

The crowd sheepishly opened for the suited warriors to enter the fray. Jeff delivered some blows of his own, before being taken down just like Rails. Ethan surrendered at once, displaying his open palms to be zip-tied, but security had more preventative measures and bound his wrists and ankles. Samantha was even roughed up but she shrugged off the calloused hands with ease, threatening a lawsuit. Suddenly, a shriek came from the entrance. The cigarettes sent a placard ablaze at the entrance, that of a budding, late-teen pop-poet from Pakistan. It was life-size, and in a matter of seconds, a pillaring flame sent tinder asunder, lighting magazines and books. The frenzied crowd darted for the entrance, piling up onto each other, trampling text and flesh. Max, who was perusing the CD's and vinyl for a long-awaited Tom Waits release, saw the charcoal smoke billowing and ducked out the emergency exit. Jeff, Samantha rose to their feet and into a crouched position poised to flee, yet saw Ethan sobbing on the ground, unable to free his restraints. Without a moment to spare, Jeff lifted his jean cuff, brandishing a fixed switchblade—which made Samantha raise an eyebrow—and sliced apart Ethan's zip-tied ankles.

"C'mon, let's roll!" Jeff shouted, high-tailing it to the CD department. The trio crouched low, covering their mouths and nudging into shelves until the plume was expulsed through the doorway. As the trio recuperated, they witnessed a disrobed Max lying on his back. He was wheezing. Tyler Young was the only casualty.

"You have got to be kidding me. Max?" Jeff said.

"Whelp, this must be like a Scooby-Doo episode's end. I am Tyler Young, have been for some time now."

"I have…so many questions to ask." Jeff said.

"There's a bar within walking distance. Y'all down? My treat for putting you through this gambit."

"Yes, you owe us," Samantha laughed. "Too bad we can't get Rails to join us—"

Firetrucks swerved into the parking lot. Lots of shouting and rushing water ensued.

"Ethan, you down to join?" Max asked. "I know we're all a little beat up, but the night is young."

He seemed hesitant at first, shivering at the fact even, yet he came to once his heart rate subsided and the adrenaline wore off.

"Why, yes I would love to."

He then offered his hand to Jeff as a token of peace. The two shook hands and the night was off to a much better start. Luckily, every customer was evacuated with only minor injuries.

Twenty-eight

The crew arrived at the packed bar. The Texas Rangers were playing and winning 4-1 over the Baltimore Orioles. Max glanced around, seeing some patrons were from the reading. Not like they would recognize him, but he shuffled from foot to foot while they waited to be seated.

"Dude, you look nervous as shit," Jeff joked.

"Yeah, because there are people here from the reading."

"Ah, they won't recognize you! You don't have that wig anymore," Samantha said. Max nodded at the assurance. "Oh, there! In the corner is a table."

They sat and a buxom female server came to them.

"Heavens, Y'all smell like a bonfire," she said jovially, handing out menus.

"Yes, quite the bonfire," Ethan Lane said. He lowered his gaze to the table bashfully. He seemed nervous talking to her pearly smile.

"What can I get you, sugar?" She started with Ethan. He blushed.

"Umm, can I have a…"

"He'll take a Rolling Rock to start!" Max said, jumping in. "Make it four, please. Tall boy's".

"You bet!"

She walked away and Max gave Ethan a playful nudge on the arm.

"Want me to work some Tyler Young magic for you? She seems nice."

"Shucks," Ethan said.

Jeff and Samantha chuckled; she pecked him on the cheek.

"How long has *this* been going on?" Max said, pointing to them.

"It was right when—"

"Oh, Max. Let me tell you how ballsy your friend was when he stood up against Stone Pony, I just ravished him. Right on the lobby floor!"

"Damn, you're a spitfire, Samantha," Max said, folding his arms and nodding his head. "You got a keeper, Jeff."

"Don't remind me," Jeff said, returning her affection.

Once the gang got their first round, Max ordered a half-rack of ribs and fries, as an appetizer. The rest of the crew split nachos. Occasionally, Max would snag a cheesy chip from the plate with barbeque sauce-laced fingers. Jeff would elbow him to remind Max of is gluttony, to which he would respond 'What? I'm hungry!' Old habits never die. Once the plates were cleared, Max ordered a pulled pork sandwich, while the rest got drinks that best suited their tastes: Jeff with a hoppy craft beer, Samantha with a Cosmo, and Ethan with a Cuba Libre. Their spirits heightened from the night's earlier events and the crowd was getting more raucous; the Rangers were leading into the 9th inning.

"So, Max, when you get a chance to breathe, tell me about this poetry gig."

"Oh, *that*?" Max said. He belched, wiping barbeque sauce from his lips with a soiled napkin. "Tonight, was stop one. My publisher bailed on me when shit started to go haywire. Doesn't matter. I made my money from the chapbook."

"Dirty pants and…?" Samantha said.

"Dirty *Panties* and Pelagius," Max emphasized. "I won't get into detail, but I subtly reveal the hypocrisy of man," He looked to Samantha. "Well, humankind, I should say. As you saw at Barney & Jules, there was quite the mix."

"You got that right. Say, why the fuck was Rails there?" Jeff said.

Max giggled. "I have no idea. But let's just say he won't be happy with me."

Samantha was on her phone and noticed the email.

"No fucking way. You're the mastermind behind all that?"

Max nodded.

"I always knew you were an outlaw," Jeff said, raising his glass. "To Tech!"

The trio raised their glasses. Ethan sat there in silence, being the oddball of the conversation.

"Cheers to the end of Glanceagram, right Ethan?" Jeff said.

"Yeah, sure," he whispered, raising his glass.

"Hey, don't feel bad, Ethan," Jeff said. "I know the whole Pollination Station thing got you down, but—"

"Whoa, whoa," Max interrupted. "*You* were behind that?"

Jeff sighed. "Sadly, yes. I broke Glanceagram with that monstrosity."

"Gee and I thought I had demons," Max said, downing the rest of his beer.

"We are a fucking crew huh?" Jeff said. He ordered another round for the table. The same server came back, eying up Ethan in his stupor.

"Why you sure are handsome with your blushing cheeks!" she said.

"Thanks. I didn't even notice."

"Y'know, I get done my shift in a half hour. Y'all still be around?"

Ethan looked at the group. They encourage him with wide eyes and smiles.

"Uh, yeah, sure! Hey, do you want my book?"

"You're a writer? Bless my stars!"

"A poet, actually," Ethan said with a smirk.

"Oh, my. Poetry makes me swoon."

Jeff winked at Ethan. The night carried on with a live rock cover band tuning up. The Rangers won, too. Samantha wanted to dance with Jeff on the parquet floor. He went reluctantly at first, then broke out some surprisingly smooth dance moves—shuffling at best. Ethan departed outside with the server, who led him outside by the arm. Max already used the bathroom twice and was looking for something to do. Now that his plan was done, and his Glanceagram account in peril of going under, he sat alone at the corner of the bar. He ordered a Moor's Light on the pretense of 'something new'.

"Yuck, tastes like shit."

The band continued to play and more people left the bar and made it to the dancefloor. Max was dozing off, so he ordered some fries. Once they arrived though, he only ate a couple before going back to his phone. He didn't realize but some fries were getting taken from someone. Once he was done, he looked up and saw the offender.

"Hi there, Tyler Young," Julie said, munching on a crispy end.

Max guffawed at the sight of the very last person he expected to see.

"Ju…Julie?" "Why are you here?"

"I saw the ads around Tech and since the Barney & Jules is currently a charred mess, I decided to go to the closest place you'd fine Rolling Rock. Jeez, Max, you put on weight, but I could still point you out like a line-up."

She kept her distance from him, leaning her torso away from his arm's reach.

"Well…your…uh, judgment, was correct," he said. His stammers were authentic; he was being pulled apart. Dark stains appeared in random areas of his shirt.

Julie continued her snide tirade. "I see that you have the ability to destroy two establishments in less than a week. You realize Waters may be on suicide watch now. And God only knows what is going on with Rails."

"It was only a simple prank."

"*Really* Max? Your definition of 'simple' is nothing short of maniacal. I'd know; I've slept with you."

"Can you please not assume the wench again? Especially here?"

"Wench?"

Julie flipped the plate of fries onto the floor. The crash was sharp and interruptive. The bartenders threw up their hands in disgust and a few people crowded around. Jeff and Samantha, who were chatting with the band on their break, also broadcasted in.

"No, Max. You get off your high horse and talk to me like a fucking equal for once. Yeah, sure, you wrote my paper, but y'know what? I still passed my semester with a 3.6 and I'm getting a scholarship at Penn because of it. You may have ruined my moment, as well as Chang, but I held firm. Maybe, if you'd thought with a clear head, you'd be joining me."

Max sat still, gulping. He was shot right in the heart. The crowd booed him.

"Oh, quiet down, you derelicts!" Max barked. The instigation continued but also beckoned Jeff and Samantha to the rescue.

"Hey. Julie, right?" Jeff said. "Let my buddy talk a minute, ok?"

"Ok, Max. Whad'ya got on me now?"

"I…just want to know one thing."

"What?"

"Are you really pregnant?"

Julie exploded in laughter, slapping the bar with an open palm.

"Nope. It was all a lie. I knew it would've been impossible to rope you in as my boyfriend by 'normal' means, so I had to go extreme, like you."

Max's face flushed.

"Julie, the reason I did *all* of that, was mostly to win you back."

Julie's eyebrows arched. "What do you mean?"

"The whole scheme was, well, my bravado showing. I had a book deal in the works, Glanceagram in the palm of my hand, and I was undermining the whole 'establishment', just to impress you. Hell, I dropped out for you!"

"Max, stop it. *Dropped out?*"

"True."

"What the fuck, man?" Jeff said. "You were so close!"

Max stomped out of the bar. Julie chased after him.

"Yo! The fucking plate, lady?" a bartender shouted. Jeff twitched for a second, dug a $20 out of his pocket, and slapped it on the bar without even looking at him.

Max and Julie were sitting in a planter in the parking lot. The tree was shielding his face from the full moon, but his tears were indiscriminate. Jeff and Samantha approached them in an intimate conversation.

"I feel so bad for them," Samantha whispered. "So much confliction."

"Ah, if only I would've known this turmoil, I'd write a novel on it," Jeff said.

"I love your foolishness, babe," she said, kissing his cheek.

"…and you know that I really had a thing for you, Max. It's just…I don't know. Maybe you're not very good at communicating."

"Ok' I'll admit. My plan possessed me. And with the ego Glanceagram gave me, it just got worse. *Way* worse."

Julie bowed her head. Max grasped her hands.

"Look, I am glad you got a scholarship. I'm bitter but happy. Bitter more so for me…for not sticking around."

Julie managed a meek smile; her teeth were white as ever.

"Well, if you think about it, aren't we all just Pelagian puppets? Just thrashing about with our 'free will' and bullshit? You chose to write my paper; I chose to have sex with you…"

"My, goodness. Hath thou swooned thee with trumpets aplenty?"

Julie chuckled at the remark and kissed him on the lips for the first time. A light breeze rustled the tree, allowing some moonlight to penetrate and engulf them.

"Y'know, Julie," Jeff called out. "He's more of an outlaw, but hey, a puppet will do. A raggedy, drunk, puppet."

Twenty-nine

Lisa Polk noticed the overstuffed envelope in her office mailbox. She had just finished writing an article on the oppression of the brown-skinned woman and its relationship to white male patriarchy that dominated society.

"What in the world?"

She stepped out of the office with the envelope in hand, darting around the floor to look for the postman; her stilettos clicked on the tile floor. She caught him around the corner and was nearing the staircase.

"Excuse me," she said. Her nose was pointed upward. "What is the meaning of this?"

"It's, uh, your package," the postman said.

"I know all my contacts who send me horrid 'snail-mail', and *this* doesn't even have a return address. It's anonymous.

The postman sighed. "Are you Lisa Polk?"

She chuckled with pretension. "Why, yes."

"Then, it is *your* package," he said, departing through the stairway door.

Lisa huffed. "Such a prickish swine, that's for sure."

Lisa had grown up with white privilege in an idyllic community of many affluent families. She had the best of everything and her parents paid for her MFA, which led to her superb editorial skills. WANK granted moderate success for her in the literary circles and Lisa was flooded daily with emails for interviews and freelance requests for national publications, like *Mental Book* and *The Bluffington Bias*. Yet, despite her blossoming career, Lisa harbored a hatred for anyone that dared to criticize her writing. Lately, she had been attacked on her Glanceagram poetry page, by a user named pelagius_fail. Lisa was astounded that others didn't like her genius sonnets and haikus she posted. In graduate school at UC Berkeley, Lisa got indoctrinated into believing tolerance was always acceptable until one disagreed with you.

"This is quite a large envelope and somebody went through a lot of trouble to mail it," Lisa thought as she opened it. She gasped at the apparent bloodstains on some pages and dropped it immediately, scouring for hand sanitizer. She paged her secretary.

"Chadwick!"

"Yes, malady?"

"Why didn't you screen this package? This is a terroristic threat!"

"Calm down, my queen," Chadwick whispered. "It looks...bodily fluid. Gross!"

"Hold on. Let me look."

Chadwick came in, wearing a black spandex bodysuit and a hot-pink tie. It was mandatory attire.

"There, see it?"

"Hmm, yes I do. It looks...like ketchup?"

"No, no! That's fucking blood. I'm not touching that shit."

Lisa paced around the office, sweating. She was about to research, 'chemical terrorism' on her smartphone when Chadwick spoke up.

"Hey, Lisa. I can just read it. I'm sure it's not dangerous."

"Fine, fine. Be the guinea pig."

Chadwick daintily picked a corner and held it forward.

"Ok. *Dear Great Whore...*" Ew, so uncouth."

"Continue!" Lisa shouted. Her scowl was akin to Satan.

"The unprovoked rebuke of myself and beloved chapbook must have made your frigid heart dance in the stench that is your putrid collective of moronic thought known as WANK and said sewer rag Pride—"

Lisa kicked the underside of the desk, driving her heel through it.

"Ahh! Wilson...Max Wilson!"

#theend

#instapoet

#wtfdidijustread

About the Authors

Thom Young is a writer from Texas. His work has been in PBS Newshour, The Wall Street Journal, The Oxford Review, University of Chicago, and over a hundred literary journals. A 2008 Million Writers Award and 2016 Pushcart Prize nominee. His work was recently featured in the *F(r)iction Magazine* in over 700 Barnes & Noble locations. You can follow him on Instagram @tyypoet

Matt Blythe is a novelist and critic born in Montana and spent a lot of time in NYC, before settling down as a caretaker of retired race horses. *Instapoet* is his first novel.

www.ingramcontent.com/pod-product-compliance
Lightning Source LLC
Chambersburg PA
CBHW06092512062 6
46557CB00003B/879

* 9 7 8 0 6 9 2 0 6 1 7 5 6 *